the Same Page

MAUREEN MARQUETTE

SAPPHIRE COLLECTIVE PUBLISHING
JACKSONVILLE, FLORIDA

First paperback edition March 2025

Book cover and interior layout designed by CMB Editing

ISBN 978-1-963340-03-7 (paperback)
ISBN 978-1-963340-09-9 (paperback)
ISBN 978-1-963340-10-5 (hardcover)
ISBN 978-1-963340-02-0 (eBook)

Published by Sapphire Collective Publishing, Jacksonville, Florida

For my mom,

who read this story and only gave me one note on page 3.

If there are any mistakes or plot holes, I blame you.

the
Same
Page

PROLOGUE

10 years ago

Selena Gallagher watched her son Neil dance in circles in front of the living room windows. Her best friend, Tabitha, had arrived and walked toward the house carrying a large box wrapped in colorful paper fit for a three-year-old little boy.

"Bis car! Bis car!" he squealed and pointed outside.

Selena opened the door with a laugh and watched as her little boy ran into Tabitha's legs. He released a goofy little giggle, one reserved only for his Aunt Bis. Selena and Tabitha's gazes met, and they broke into twin grins. The little boy's silliness always put them in a good mood, though it was hard not to be when they were within one another's company.

"Hey, Little Bit," Tabitha said, passing the hefty box to Selena before kneeling in front of the three-year-old.

Neil jumped and wrapped his little arms around her neck. He talked excitedly into her neck, but the only words Selena could make out were "Bis," "car," and "cake," and that was only because she spent all her time with him. Mothers understood their children, even when they didn't make a lick of sense to anyone else. Selena never would have expected Tabitha to understand him, but she joined in his conversation without skipping a beat.

"Now that I'm here, I can help with that," she said with an open smile.

Neil pulled back and nodded, his expression turned downright serious. He placed his hand on her cheek, and Selena felt a tiny jab in her heart, like an intruder on something so intimate, a friendship so pure. There was such love between the two, and it made her heart explode with happiness. Selena had worried having a child would cause tension between her and Tabitha after hearing horror stories of others who had lost touch with friends after having children. But Neil only seemed to bring them closer, and Tabitha relished having the title of Aunt Bis.

"Come on in." Selena gestured toward the house, and little Neil took Tabitha's hand and dragged her inside.

"Thanks." Tabitha offered Selena an air kiss on her way past, falling in line behind the little man. "I'll find you after we save the world from alien dinosaur robots. Or until another kiddo arrives and distracts him. Though it'll be difficult to tear himself away from me, I will do my best to encourage socialization within his peer group. I won't let him neglect the other kids just because I'm the most interesting person ever."

With a shake of her head, Selena brought the gift to the dining room table. The house was decorated with aliens, dinosaurs, and robots, because Neil couldn't decide which he'd rather have for his third birthday party. Aliens and aircraft hung from the ceiling, and dinosaur backgrounds hung down the walls, and robots Selena built from cardboard boxes and paint were placed around the room.

Walking down the stairs with his eyes glued in a book, Selena's husband Bo almost walked right into her. When he realized, he stopped, lowered the book, and gave her a flirty grin.

"Hello, Gorgeous." He leaned forward, granting her with a soul-searing kiss.

She purred against him. "You might want to put the book away until after the party. I need your undivided attention to help wrangle the kids. I can't do it all by myself."

"Have Tabitha help. She's good with them." He tucked a bookmark to keep his page and closed the book.

"She has no patience for kids."

Tabitha crawled into the living room from Neil's bedroom, the little boy dragging beside her with his arms wrapped around her neck. She spoke in clicks like an alien while Neil growled like a dinosaur.

"Your puny dinosaur brain is no match for my alien intelligence," Tabitha then said in a robotic voice. "Get the dinosaurs. Get the dinosaurs." She reached for Neil, who barked out a laugh and ran around the sofa to get away.

"Yeah, you're right," Bo said, giving Selena the side eye. "She's horrible with children."

Selena gave him an exasperated look and shook her head,

hiding a smirk. Though Tabitha did really well with Neil, Selena knew she didn't have the patience or energy to spend much time around other children. In fact, if Tabitha ever decided to have her own kids, Selena would be very surprised indeed.

The doorbell rang, stealing away Selena's chance at a rebuttal, and the birthday party officially began.

***

Selena sighed as the door closed behind the last of the partygoers. Entertaining the screaming toddlers and their judgmental parents had left her emotionally raw. She hated having to bend over backwards for parents who demanded their children eat a gluten free diet without an allergy or who refused to allow their child to act like a child. She struggled just to feel like she was raising a happy and healthy child.

"That went well," Bo said, slipping his arms around Selena from behind. He nuzzled into her neck with a soft brush of his lips.

"I think so, too." She turned around in his arms, looping

hers around his neck, and stood on her tiptoes for a kiss. When she pulled back, she noticed Tabitha over Bo's shoulder, her face pulled taut into a deep frown, the color in her face as pale as the moon. "You alright? You look off."

Selena crossed the room, slipping from Bo's reach, and felt for her friend's forehead, but Tabitha retreated. "Are you sick?"

"I'm moving to New York," Tabitha blurted, avoiding eye contact, and began gathering her belongings.

The words hit Selena like a punch to the stomach. Her best friend was leaving her, and she had no clue it was even an idea in Tabitha's head.

"But you've always wanted to stay here in town," she pled, grasping Tabitha's shoulders. Selena hoped, if she shook hard enough, she could knock some sense into her best friend. "What happened to starting your own fashion line and opening a boutique right next door to my bakery? We have a plan."

"I have to move. It's... it's for my career. No designer ever did anything with their life if they didn't work in New York City or Paris." Tabitha grabbed her hands and held them between the two friends. "Tell me you understand, that you're happy for me.

Please? I don't think I could actually do it if I didn't know I'd still have you."

Though she didn't want to, Selena nodded, giving Tabitha her blessing. She couldn't stand in the way of her best friend's happiness. It would kill her being so far away, but Selena had faith in their friendship. They could make it through anything.

CHAPTER 1

Tabitha McElmore entered the sewing room, which had 23 sewing machines stationed around the perimeter of the room and bored models donning next autumn's fall fashions while crazed designers fluttered around them making last minute alterations. She handed off a bolt of heavyweight duchess satin to one of her staff so he could add an interior slip layer for the dress his model wore. Her eyebrows knitted as she noticed the gown hanging awkwardly from the model's bony shoulders.

"The boat neckline isn't working on that." She scrunched her nose in thought. An idea formed as she dove deeper into the room but she called back over her shoulder to the seamstress blankly staring at it. "Brigitte, make that a deep-V. It'll make the bodice pop and draw the eyeline downward. The whole ensemble will come together."

Her fingers fixed a twisted strap on another model's shoulder, and her eyes swept across the beading along the neckline. Perfect, she thought.

A phone ringing entered her consciousness, but she ignored it. Knowing it wasn't hers, because everyone knew not to bother her when a show was around the corner, she continued down the row of ensembles she and the label were preparing for the spring fashion week in Milan, Italy.

"Tabby cat. You hear that? That's you, baby girl," said Frances, one of her favorite assistant designers.

With a frown, she pulled the iPhone from her back pocket, and surprise washed over her when she noticed the name. Neil.

"Hi, Little Bit. I know we have our weekly chat tonight, but..." she said, gesturing silent directions to Frances to shorten the hemline in the front of his model's tunic. Though it wasn't her favorite, the high/low cut was back. Another designer caught her attention, so she cut through the room. "I'm a little busy right now. Can I call you back?"

"Bis..."

She stopped short, and whichever minion was following her bumped into her, hard, turning her around with the force.

"What's wrong?" she demanded, hearing the emotion in the one word that Neil was trying to suppress but failed.

"It's the bakery. I think... I think we're going to lose it. Dad's been... He hasn't..." The young man growled, refusing to speak ill of his father. He sighed deeply, wearily. "We got a final notice in the mail, and I'm worried."

"Is he okay?" Her heart stopped. She had been lifelong friends with Bo, until damn near twenty years ago he'd first gotten together with her best friend. He still held a soft spot in her heart, though it would be a cold day in hell before she ever admitted that. It was easier if everyone, including him, especially him, thought their relationship had just grown tumultuous over the years. Nobody needed to know just how much she cared.

"He's not doing well. Neither am I." His voice was shaky when he said, "Bis, I need you. We both do."

Tabitha spotted her boss, the Antonio Riviera Fashion

House's namesake designer, enter the crowded room and spoke into the phone as she stalked to the entrance. "I'll take care of it, Neil. I promise."

Hanging up the phone, she interrupted Antonio's instruction to one of the seamstresses.

"Antonio, I have to leave."

"Alright, Love, but make sure you catch the plane to Milan in the morning." He said without glancing in her direction.

"I won't make it. There's a family emergency, and... I have to go home."

His posture straightened, and he faced her slowly, his lips puckering in thought. "Home to little Saint Jerry, Georgia?"

"Saint Joshua."

"Doesn't matter. It's all the same." He huffed, hands untangling her words in the air. "You know what you're risking with this request?"

She nodded. Everything she had worked hard for over the last ten years was at stake. If she didn't go to Milan, didn't present her own designs and left Antonio and the team to do it themselves, she could be detrimentally hurting her career.

But Neil needed her. There wasn't anything she wouldn't do for that boy. Her work, her designs, her career... be damned.

"You'll return when?"

"I don't know." She bit her lip. This was an unusual request and one of the worst times of year to make it.

Antonio inhaled long and slow, releasing it the same way. "Brigitte, dust off your passport. You're going to Milan tomorrow." He shooed Tabitha away with a gentle swoop of his hand and glided over to the next designer.

A pit stirred in Tabitha's stomach as she pulled up her favorite travel site in her phone to change her plans.

***

When Tabitha arrived at the airport in Jacksonville the next day, she rented a car and drove the short distance north into Saint Joshua, Georgia. She had always loved her town. It was a small coastal town that gave her the feeling of home and being known. When she was in New York, she really only had one friend, and that was because they'd met outside of work. No one else really knew her or was even interested in getting to know her, only the persona she created to succeed in such a challenging job market. Everyone wanted to make it big in fashion, and they were all willing to go the extra mile to get there—sometimes resorting to sabotage. Tabitha had had to put on a façade to get ahead of the pack.

But life wasn't like that here. They weren't like that here. In Saint Joshua, Tabitha was the girl who punched a boy for picking on her best friend when she was ten, the teenager who pined after the boy next door, the woman who wanted to do big things and left only to do them.

Often, she wondered if she was failing Neil by being away so much, especially since Selena's passing almost three years ago. She should have moved back then, should have been here to help him and Bo in their time of need. But she didn't. She was already struggling with the loss of her best friend in addition to her own recent divorce. She didn't have anything left in her to guide two others struggling through their loss, as well.

As the town came into view, a smile broke out across her face. Though things changed over time, they generally stayed the same. Meers Grocery may have gotten a facelift, but she would have bet money they still offered a discount to the sheriff's office employees, donated the food nearing its expiration date, and Margery Owens worked checkout lane 3. There were just some things you could count on, and Saint Joshua was one of them.

Tabitha turned onto Maple, wanting to pass the Moon Pie Bakery on her way to the Gallagher house. It was closed, so she couldn't stop in to see Alice Dumbowski, the manager, but she wanted to check in on the place. Neil had sounded worried.

It didn't look any different from the outside. The old brick building appeared the same it always had. The name of the bakery hung above the large front window that was framed with white molding, which if she was being honest, could use a paint job. People walked right past, without even a glance toward the building. It was later in the day, and the shop was already closed, but the societal neglect gave her pause. Did anyone remember it anymore? Did anybody shop there anymore? Was that what Neil meant when he said they might lose it?

All the questions floating around her head wouldn't be solved staring at an empty building, so she drove until she pulled into the driveway of a house she knew very well.

This one, though unchanged in every way, didn't give her a feeling of hope like the rest of the town gave her. Memories of pain and loss came flooding back. She'd spent a lot of time here over the years. Hell, she'd even helped with the painting and decorating. Despite the onslaught of memories, she had to go inside. If not for Neil, then for Selena. Her best friend's legacy was at stake.

She wound her way up to the front door and knocked since the doorbell had been broken for as long as they lived there. Nobody answered. She tried again, and when the door remained firmly closed, she found the correct key on her ring and opened the door herself.

An overwhelming musk hit her like a pile of bricks, a combination of teenage boy and the odor of a house that hadn't been dusted or aired out in a really long time. She stepped back and breathed some fresh air before she could attempt another venture inside the dark house. Only the diminishing sunlight from outside illuminated the rooms through cracks between the window slats.

"Hello?" she called. "Is anybody home?"

A noisy racket came from upstairs, so she called out again.

"Neil? Bo? Anyone there?"

The sound of someone running down the second-floor hallway gave her unease until the sight of Neil pouncing down the stairwell came into sight. He barreled into her, hugging her tightly around the neck.

"You came!"

He was taller than she remembered. It wouldn't be long before he would overtake her own 5'4" stature.

"You sound surprised. You know I'll always be here for you." There was nothing that would have stopped her.

"I know," he sniffed. "But still... I wasn't sure you'd come."

She ruffled his hair and looked around the house. It definitely needed someone, and she was here now. She'd have to make sure to clean up and air it out before she flew home.

"Where's your dad? He didn't leave you here alone, did he?" She craned her neck to investigate the living room on one side of the foyer then the study on the other.

"No," he said, ducking his head. "He's in his office."

Tabitha's gaze travelled up, as if she could see through the ceiling to Bo's office on the second floor. She patted Neil's arm before venturing up the stairs and knocking on the door to the third bedroom, which they had converted to Bo's personal writing space seven years ago. After receiving no response, she pushed the door open and let the waft of body odor, Scotch, and shame filter out.

Bo's head rested on loose sheets of paper spread across the desk. Drool had pooled on several of them, and others were filled with scratches of red ink. A pile of crumpled sheets overflowed from the trash can beside the desk, and an empty bottle lay beside his face.

Of all the things she expected to find when she arrived, it was so much worse.

Enough was enough, she thought, turning on her heel. She retrieved a bucket from under the bathroom sink, filled it with as cold of water as she could get from the shower, and dumped it over his head. From the state of things, she was in no mood to go easy on this man. He needed a wake-up call, and she was just the person for the job.

"What the hell?" he shouted, scrambling away from the desk. His gaze snagged on her, and his expression turned thunderous. "Bis? What the fuck are you doing here? And what was that for? You could have killed me! Waterboarding is illegal!" He gestured to the desk, and the sight took a moment to register in his brain. "Look at all my work. You've ruined it!" He reached for the soaking papers at the desk, trying to separate them from one another, but to no avail.

She walked across the room and slid up both windows, leaving them wide open. As the cool breeze came in, she finally got another whiff of fresh air. Her lungs were thankful for the reprieve.

"This place is disgusting. You are rank and in desperate need of a shower. That boy looks like he hasn't had a decent meal in three years. You're about to lose the bakery, the place my best friend always dreamed of opening. And this house is a pigsty. What the fuck do you think I'm doing here? Did you think I wouldn't find out about any of this?"

"This is none of your business," he growled, storming out of the office.

"Yes, it is. Of course, it's my business," she said, following behind him. "I loved Selena more than you could ever know! She was like my sister. I will not stand by as you ruin her legacy like this."

"Go away, Tabitha," he said, his voice venomous. "You don't belong here, and nobody wants you here." He slammed the door to the bathroom shut in her face.

Yep, she thought, there was no place like home...

CHAPTER 2

As Bo Gallagher peeled off his soaking t-shirt, he groaned at his reflection in the bathroom. "Who does she think she is? Coming in and taking over likes she owns the place," he muttered to himself.

He had been friends with Tabitha when they were younger, but she'd grown colder toward him as the years passed. He never learned what caused the drift. It was like one day, they were friends, almost as close as Tabitha and Selena were, and the next, he was expelled from her life. He really didn't understand her sudden arrival. She couldn't be there to see him, so she must have flown in to visit her parents and just came over to see Neil. He could put up with her meddling for an afternoon before she went back to ignoring his existence.

Gazing into the mirror, he sneered at the sight of harsh red lines marring his face, transfer from the pen markings across his work. He had edited the life and emotion out of everything he'd been able to write in the last three years. His publisher denied the last full manuscript he was able to churn out, and he hadn't been able to write anything noteworthy since. Every word he put on paper was as lifeless as the plants left behind after Selena was no longer around to care for them. He threw them away when he stumbled across them over the years. He never realized how many plants she had kept indoors and was still randomly finding pots filled with death.

He washed away the ink lines, slipped his robe on to cover his now naked torso, and returned to his office, where his phone began ringing as he entered.

"You missed another deadline, Gallagher," his agent hollered at him the moment he answered the phone.

Schuyler West was a ballbuster, which was why he'd chosen her for his first novel. She reminded him of someone, though he couldn't pinpoint who exactly. She knew what she wanted, when she wanted, and was not afraid to ask for it. If she wanted a book based during the Civil War, she told him. If she wanted a story re-written into first person, rather than third, she demanded it. She had a keen sense of what worked, and he trusted her.

But he couldn't make words appear when he had nothing to say. And any time he tried putting pen to paper, he felt like a phony.

"I know." He sighed looking at the mess of papers on his desk. Though he yelled at Tabitha for ruining them, the truth was they had nothing on them worth ruining. "I got nothing."

He had tried being an action writer, telling stories of spies and bad guys and saving the world. Schuyler had taken him on as a client but couldn't get anything of his sold to a publisher. She suggested he write in a different genre to get a better scope of his skills. His response was to tell the story of him and Selena and how they fell in love. It sold immediately, and he became the next Nicholas Sparks, but without all the tragic endings. He'd been writing romance novels ever since. But lately, there were no sto-ries floating around his head that would fall under that genre. His inspiration had died with his muse.

Schuyler groaned. "What did I tell you? If you're having a block, tell me. We can work out the story together."

"You don't get it... There is no story."

She fell silent for a beat. "You mean to tell me your book is scheduled to be published in six months and there is no book?"

He cringed at her clipped words, each enunciated carefully. "That's exactly the issue, Sky."

She swore and hung up the phone.

He stared at his cell and tapped it against his chin. Without a story, he would have to return his advance. He hadn't paid attention to the finances lately, but they'd be alright without it. After all, he had plenty from his last book-to-film adaptation. Most people didn't know it, but authors rarely made much money writing stories. Selling the film rights was how most made the big bucks. He nearly shit himself when he saw the payment from the production company when filming began. He'd taken Selena to Ireland as a thanks for taking care of him, Neil, and the house while he wrote. But now, she was gone, and so were his words.

His phone rang in his hand. Schuyler again. "Yeah?"

"I bought you three months, but if you don't have something approved by then, you have to return the advance. And take note, you have to return all of it, including my cut. That does not come out of my pocket, you hear me?"

"Yeah, but what if.."

"Don't."

"I'm just saying..."

"I know what you're saying, Gallagher, but don't. You have another story in you. I know you do. If you want to quit after that, fine. But you are fulfilling your contract. I'll be calling every day until you send me something. Am I clear?"

"Yes, ma'am." He groaned and rubbed his free hand over his face. He never did well on a deadline. He always got all anxious, and then the words got blocked up in his mind.

"You sound like shit. You alright?"

"Course."

"How's Neil? You caring for that boy?" Her words sounded off, like she was genuinely concerned he wouldn't be taking care of his son.

He groaned again, knowing Neil took way better care of him. "He's fine. Tabitha's here."

"Good," she said. "I like her. Maybe she can get on your ass when I can't. Help you knock out some pages."

"It's always bothered me how well you two got along."

"Don't fight it," she said. He could hear the smirk in her voice. "Get to work. I'll check in tomorrow."

"Looking forward to it," he said, hanging up the phone without a goodbye, but the line had already gone dead. She was never one for goodbyes anyhow.

He tossed the phone onto the desk, quickly picked it back up, remembering the water, and slipped it into his robe pocket. He ambled into the hallway linen closet, grabbed a few towels, and soaked up the mess, tossing out the whole stack of papers. There was nothing good in them anyway.

He brought the damp towels downstairs to put them in the laundry room but stopped at the entrance to the kitchen. Tabitha was inside with Neil, singing and laughing as they made a mess at the stove. When she began singing Frank Sinatra, he felt the tears welling up inside himself. Selena loved Sinatra. She loved him so much that Fly Me to the Moon was their song, the one they danced to on their wedding day, their first dance. It was theirs—

his and hers. It felt wrong to hear Tabitha singing it.

"Make sure to clean up after yourselves in there," he lashed out, storming away to hide his pain.

While he couldn't make out the exact words, he heard Tabitha mumble something under her breath. He knew in his gut it wasn't kind.

"We're just making dinner," Neil said.

His son's voice was meek, and Bo hated being the reason for whatever emotion was there. He loved his son, but he couldn't seem to do anything right by him lately. He was failing as a father, as a writer, as a person. Nothing he did or said was right anymore, not since Selena passed.

When she was alive, he always had the right words, made people feel loved and cherished, and always felt that in return. Things weren't like that anymore, and he didn't know how to get back on track. It was like she had the playbook and coached him to do the right thing. He was flailing without her and could no longer find the right plays.

After stuffing the dirty towels into the washer and starting the cycle, he pulled his phone out of his robe. He pulled up his best friend's name and waited for it to connect.

"Gallagher, it's been a while. How you been?" said Glenn Dumbowski when he picked up. They'd been friends all their lives, and Glenn know specifically how much he'd been struggling without Selena.

"Tabitha's here."

"Why, man? What brings that beautiful woman 'round your house? If I knew she would be in town, I'd have offered her my spare room."

"Dunno, man. She just showed up. Help me get her out of my house. I'm afraid I may kill her if she stays any longer."

Glenn laughed, and Bo could hear Glenn's eyes rolling. "What's up your ass? If I'm scared for anyone, it's for you. That girl could take you any day of the week."

That's what worried him. She was headstrong and independent and could take care of herself. No matter what he did to get rid of her, she gave as good as she got. Better even. He'd be stuck with her until she decided she was ready to leave.

Thinking of how much of a spitfire she was resurfaced a memory from high school. Tommy Mercer had been harassing her, trying to get her to agree to a date, but she'd stood her ground, not taking any of his shit. She was yelling at him so thoroughly, and the entire school had witnessed it. The only reason Bo stepped in was because Mercer appeared close to crying, and he didn't want the man's reputation to be ruined forever. Tommy would have doubled down on his harassment of Tabitha, making her life horrible had she damaged his ego like that. But Tabitha had seen Bo's stepping in as him saving her, when really it was the other way around. He knew she could take care of herself.

"This isn't a joke. She came in and dumped a bucket of water all over my book."

Glenn was silent for a good long moment. "You're writing again?" His friend's voice held a note of something Bo wished he still had—hope.

"That's not the point. She barged in, uninvited I might add, and ruined everything I'd been working on."

"Doesn't sound like she ruined much," Glenn said with a chuckle. "What's she doing now?"

"Making dinner with Neil." Bo looked around the corner, hoping to catch a glimpse of them in the kitchen.

"Good, when was the last time that boy had a nice home-cooked meal? She's not there to mess things up, man. Just let her be and stay out of her way." His voice sobered by the time he spoke again. "She loves that boy, more than anything. Give her time to convince herself you're not irrevocably screwing him up and let her spoil him for a few days until she goes home. He deserves to be cared for."

"You think I don't take care of my son?"

"Do you?"

Bo's knee jerk reaction was to shout that he did, in fact, take care of him, but when he really thought about it, he realized he hadn't. Not for a long time. With all his own pain and suffering the past three years, he had stopped being there for Neil. He'd left Neil to practically raise himself.

That had to change.

"No, I guess not," he said resigned.

"So what are you going to do about it?" Glenn asked before hanging up on him.

That was the question of the day.

CHAPTER 3

Tabitha awoke in her childhood bedroom. It had been years since she'd been there, but the room was just as she'd left it. Her parents used it as a guest bedroom over the last fifteen years, but they didn't find a need to redecorate. She was left looking at the old Backstreet Boys poster she'd hung in the early 2000s.

She remembered jamming out to them and having lip syncing concerts at more than one slumber party with Selena, and the memory made her chuckle. It was nice when that happened. Even now, three years after the fact, most memories of her best friend made her tear up and put her in a funk for the rest of the day. But this was a good memory. Each slumber party had practically been the same, a repeat almost every weekend, but the girls had enjoyed each and every one.

While both Tabitha and Selena were just children, Selena had found her home stuffy and claustrophobic, so they usually hung out over at Tabitha's house. Being an adult in her childhood bedroom had Tabitha reliving ten years of slumber parties all at once. It was a strange experience to feel both extremely happy and overwhelmingly sad at the same time, so she let the feelings consume her while they lasted.

On several occasions, particularly as high school neared its end and Selena began dating Bo, the girls would perform their concerts for him through their bedroom windows. Tabitha had grown up next door to him, which was how they became friends in the first place, but he seemed to have eyes only for her best friend.

She sighed and tossed an arm over her face, trying to block out the memories as all the good times filtered into sad ones. There were other things she could be doing instead of wallowing in misery, like checking out the bakery, and she couldn't do that if she strolled down Memory Lane.

After crawling out of bed and taking a quick shower, she dressed in a simple outfit of high-waisted skinny jeans and a black cowl-neck sweater and descended the stairs for some coffee. Her father had already left for work, but her mother was busy at her sewing machine, probably making the costumes for the high school's spring play in the makeshift craft area in what used to be a breakfast nook. She had converted it for all her projects after Tabitha had moved away.

"Morning," Tabitha said, patting her mom's shoulder as she passed behind her.

"Good morning, Sweetheart. There're some waffles in the freezer and coffee in the pot. Help yourself."

"Thanks, Mom."

Tabitha set about making her coffee while the toaster worked its magic and set her plate on the island when everything was prepared. She settled on one of the bar stools and watched her mother hard at work. Her mom was the one who taught her to sew and design clothes. Tabitha was always grateful for the lessons that helped her achieve her goals.

"Hey, Mom?"

"Hmm?"

"Did you ever want to make your own designs?"

That got her mother's attention. Her mom's face scrunched up while she gave the question serious consideration. "I don't think I ever did, no. I used to make you clothes sometimes, when you were a child, but those were all from stencils and patterns. I've never really thought about designing anything."

Tabitha nodded, understanding that not everyone had the same passion for things others did. She knew that well. "I was just wondering. I think you'd be good at that."

Her mother's thoughtful expression burst into a blinding smile. "Thank you, Sweetheart. I take that as the highest compliment, coming from my superstar fashion designer."

Tabitha rolled her eyes, but she couldn't hide the smile. Her parents had always been her biggest fans. They were the ones who convinced her to move to New York in the first place. If it hadn't been for them and their unwavering support, she wouldn't be working at a top design house.

"If you ever decide to move to the city, I'd hire you in a heartbeat," Tabitha said.

Her mother's eyes lit with amusement as she returned to the frock she was making. "I'll keep that in mind the next time your father goes hunting and decides to use my bathtub to process his deer."

***

After some quality time with her mother, Tabitha found her way to downtown Saint Joshua. Though it was still morning, nobody was stopping at the Moon Pie. She frowned with disappointment. Every time she visited while Selena ran the place, there'd always been a steady flow of traffic coming and going. Selena had removed the bell hanging from the door because it rang just too often. But there was nobody now.

She pulled on the door handle and stepped into the cool room, the bell above the door ringing. Her brows furrowed as she glanced at it, wondering who put it back up. The lighting in the spacious room was beautiful, especially through the front-facing window. But every table was empty, and nobody stood behind the counter, which concerned her.

"I'll be right with you," Mrs. Dumbowski shouted from the kitchen.

"No need to rush, Mrs. D. It's just me," she called, making her way to the front counter display case.

Everything looked tasty, but they didn't have the look of Selena's. Her best friend always took so much care to make each treat look perfect, which meant she had a lot of rejected leftovers for her boys. Selena had refused to sell anything she deemed subpar.

"Get your skinny butt over here," Mrs. D said, making her way out from the kitchen on her short legs and waving a dish towel in Tabitha's direction. "There is no just about you."

Tabitha smiled at the older woman and returned the embrace. Getting a hug from this woman was like eating one of Selena's treats or eating soup on a chilly day. There was something so reassuring about it—perfect comfort in two bulbous arms.

"I missed you," Tabitha admitted, overwhelmed with the emotion seeing this woman stirred. "I should have been around more."

"Nonsense," Mrs. D tsked, smacking her arm with the towel.

"You've been through a lot. I would be worried if you'd been here all the time, though I sure am glad to see you now..." Her words fell away as she took in the sight of Tabitha's body. "Look at you! You're wasting away. Come, come. You need to eat something."

The older woman set out a plate and placed a white chocolate muffin on top. That was one of Tabitha's favorite, and the old woman knew it. Tabitha sat on a counter stool while Mrs. D filled two coffee mugs and slid one across the counter.

"How's life in New York?" the old woman asked, blowing over her steaming mug.

"It's good. My boss included several of my designs in the fall line during this month's fashion weeks. He also said I could include some in the spring fashion lines in September, though that was before I had to come home. I hope he still lets me."

Tabitha bit her lip. She hadn't considered Antonio wouldn't let her designs into the spring lines. Did she lose out on the opportunity because something personal came up?

"I'm sure it'll all work out, dear." Mrs. D laid her gentle hand over Tabitha's and smiled tenderly. "Any boyfriends? Or girlfriends? I worry about you being all alone up there."

Tabitha rolled her eyes. She had stopped looking for Mr. Right. She knew why she hadn't found him, despite having walked down the aisle a few times herself. It was too late for her. She didn't even have to wonder why she was in her 30s and divorced three times. She'd already missed her chance for a happy ever after; they never even stood a chance.

"No, I'm really just focusing on my career," Tabitha explained and took a sip of the coffee, that tasted off, though she was sure was the same brand and flavor Selena had served.

"Yes, but sometimes you just need a good lay."

Tabitha spit out her coffee onto the counter and stared at the old woman. She wondered what Mrs. D was like when she was younger and came to the conclusion they probably would have been friends. Very good friends.

"True, but I've been married too many times already. I'm done with men for a good, long while."

"Honey, you just need to find the right one." Mrs. D winked. "Maybe someone will catch your eye now that you're home."

Tabitha indulged the woman with a tight smile, and the bell above the door rang out. Before she could see who entered, two burly arms wrapped her in a big bear hug.

"Tabitha Grace McElmore, as I live and breathe. I heard you were back in town, and I'm so glad it's true," Glenn said, holding her with a smothering brotherly embrace.

Even when she'd kept secrets from Selena, Glenn had known exactly what was in Tabitha's heart of hearts, the only one who knew all her secrets, and had thankfully kept them all these years. He truly was one of a kind.

"Glenn Matthew Dumbowski," she laughed, turning in his arms to return his embrace.

Now that he was divorced, she wished she could feel something for him, but alas, there had never been that charge of electricity between them. She loved him, like she had loved all her husbands, but her love for Glenn was missing the same ingredient as her marriages—heat, passion, spark. Only one guy ever made her feel that way, but he'd only had that for someone else, which strictly relegated her to the friend zone. It was a shame, really, she mused. Glenn was attractive, alarmingly so, but she couldn't make something appear from nowhere. If she could, she'd still be married.

Glenn pulled back with a devastating grin. "I hear you're already making Bo miserable."

"It's his fault, really. He should want to stay on my good side." She lowered her gaze, hoping to avoid the knowing look he was sure to give her.

"He always did have a way of riling you up."

She fought against it, but her eyes met his gaze anyway. There was something in them, something she hadn't seen cast in her direction in years, something that made her insides roil in shame. He had a way of cutting through all her bullshit and getting to the heart of the matter with just one look.

"Don't go there," she said, voice cracking through emotion. She hadn't let herself indulge those thoughts, and Glenn bringing it up wouldn't do her any good. She was home to take care of Neil and get the bakery back on its feet. "How's the single life treating you nowadays? You staying out of trouble?"

Tabitha was glad for Glenn's recent divorce. His ex-wife had been toxic, not only toward Glenn, but their daughter Gracie, too. Not everybody could have a marriage like any of hers, ones based on respect and friendship, if not love. Then again, none of hers had lasted, so she clearly hadn't known what made a good marriage either.

"Of course." He winked at her. He had always been a flirt, but they both knew nothing would ever form between them. Her heart was too far gone for that, and his had become too bitter and jaded by his ex. "Mom's been helping out with Gracie, though she's been killing herself between working here and helping at home. She honestly does way too much and seriously needs to take a break, but she won't listen to me."

Mrs. D running herself ragged to care for everything, when she didn't need to be, twisted Tabitha's heart. She caught the old woman's gaze and found a guilty expression there. The old woman looked down and away, wringing her hands in front of her. She looked miserable.

"You want to quit." The realization hit Tabitha like a Mack truck.

"No, dear," Mrs. D sputtered. "I would never give up on this bakery."

"I know." She looked around at the place her best friend built. Everything looked so Selena. This was Tabitha's responsibility, not Mrs. D's. She had to own up to it. She looked Mrs. D square in the eyes and gave her the news. "You're fired."

"What?" Mrs. D balked, taken aback.

"You've been taking care of this place for way too long, and you know you'd rather spend your time with that precious grand-baby of yours." Tabitha gave her a look, one that suggested she could try arguing but wouldn't win. "I'm back, for now. I can look after the place, at least until we find a more permanent solution, though I'd appreciate it if you taught me how to bake before you leave."

The old woman began crying in relief and wrapped Tabitha in her arms again. She herself almost began tearing up. However, when she glanced over to Glenn, he was fuming. Without a final word, he stormed out of the store.

She didn't know what had just happened and hoped it wouldn't come back to bite her in the ass. She loved the Moon Pie Bakery but didn't know the first thing about running it, though Mrs. D wouldn't leave her out to dry. Tabitha could always call if she had a question or needed help.

CHAPTER 4

o stared into his son's bedroom, taking in the differences that had taken root over the last three years. Band posters hung on every wall, as well as several for professional sports teams. When did he become a Jaguars fan? There were books stacked on every flat surface, and clothes littered the floor. The last time Bo had really taken notice of the room was when Selena passed away. At the time, Disney Pixar posters had been plastered over the walls, and action figures lined the bookshelves.

He walked into the room and picked up a well-worn, well-loved copy of The Count of Monte Cristo laying on the bedside table, a bookmark about two-thirds through. Recognizing the copy, he flipped to the inside front cover page, where it read, in curly black ink: Property of Selena Cruz.

A tear slipped down his cheek. He wiped it away and fought through the pain. Neil needed him now, and from the looks of it, Bo didn't know his son anymore. The young man had grown up without him noticing. He had to change that. He had to fix their relationship. He had to become the parent Selena had always been.

The front door slammed shut, the sound of it echoing up the stairs.

"Bo, you son of a bitch!"

He recognized the voice of his best friend but had no idea the reason for the anger. He didn't have to wait long before Glenn found him seconds later, though he'd almost stormed right past on the way to Bo's office. Glenn looked at the door, as if verifying exactly where in the house they were. When the confusion settled, a furious expression took its place.

"You get that girl to go home," Glenn shouted, pointing in Bo's face. "Whatever you do, do not let her give up everything to cover for your dumb ass."

"Huh? What are you talking about? Who?" Bo's brow crinkled.

"Tabitha, you idiot. You can't let her stay, not like this."

"I don't even want her to stay," Bo argued.

"That's what I'm saying!" Glenn growled and ran his hands through his shaggy hair. He took a few breaths to calm himself before speaking again. "That girl gives up everything for this family. You cannot let her do it again! Not now that she's finally got her life and career on track."

"I can't control her. Nobody can."

"But you can close that bakery." Glenn's expression transformed from fury to sympathy at the words that carelessly flew from his mouth. "I know you don't want to, like you're keeping Selena alive by keeping it open, but... it's not making any money, and you can't allow Tabitha to stay to run a failing business. When it fails, and it will, she will blame herself. And you know that. Don't do that to the poor girl. She's been through way too much to go through losing that, too."

Bo stormed from the room, not wanting to hear what Glenn had to say, despite how much of it was truth. He desperately wanted to keep the bakery going, have Selena's dream live on, but knew it couldn't stay open forever. It wasn't feasible, and Mrs. D was only getting older. She couldn't run it for much longer. He'd have to find a more permanent solution if he wanted to keep it going.

The realization of what Glenn said struck him. He flung around to confront Glenn, but he'd followed him into the hallway, so they collided. "Why would Tabitha be running the bakery?"

"Bis fired my mom so she could finally retire." Glenn leaned against the door frame behind him.

"She doesn't have the power to fire your mom," he huffed.

Glenn crossed his arms in a defiant manner. "And yet, she did it. Mom's been wanting to retire for a while now, but she didn't want to bring it up and depress you. The bakery needs to close, Gallagher. It's time."

Bo's heart contorted in his chest. His jaw lowered, as if it knew he should say something, but he couldn't find the words.

Glenn met his gaze and squeezed his shoulder. "Just... think about it, okay?"

"Yeah, man." Bo nodded.

After Glenn left, it was all Bo could think about. And the

more he thought about it, the angrier he became. How dare she come back and butt into every aspect of his life? Tabitha had no right to make decisions for him. When the anger hit a pinnacle, he set his sights on the bakery to confront Tabitha.

He drove on auto-pilot, fury fueling his journey. He stormed inside the moment he arrived, the scent of vanilla assaulting his senses the moment the door opened. Tabitha stood behind the counter, nodding along to directions from Mrs. D on how to work the cash register, an antique register Selena had demanded they get. Seeing the joy on the old woman's face dulled his ire, but he had enough brewing that it could wait for when he could get Tabitha alone. The advantage came sooner than he expected when the Mrs. D noticed his arrival.

"Bo, dear, have you heard the great news!" she announced. "I'm finally retiring."

"I heard," he said with clipped words and a curt nod toward Tabitha. "May we speak?"

Mrs. D frantically straightened everything around them, patting the flour off her hands and apron, and rounded the counter. "I think I'll take a walk. Give you two some time to discuss...

things." With a warm kiss on his cheek, she scooted out the door.

He inhaled slowly, an attempt to temper his words, but they had a mind of their own. "What. The hell. Were you thinking? You can't swoop into town and fire my employees. You do not have the right."

"Actually, I do." She came around the counter and crossed her arms, gearing up for the fight he provoked. He should have known she wouldn't just let him yell without giving as much as she got. "I am an investor, which makes me part owner. And since you haven't been taking care of this place, I will."

Stomping across the room, he scowled down at her. "Who says I haven't been caring for this place? Mrs. D works really hard to keep it open."

They stood only a foot apart, anger creating palpable tension in the space between them. Her breathing quickened as a bright red flush started on her chest and spread up to her cheeks. Her anger showed rather quickly, but she was nowhere near the point of giving up. He'd found he was the only person who could rile her up this quickly, and damned if he wasn't proud of that fact.

"For free! You're not even paying her," she shouted back.

He took a step back when her words hit home. "What do you mean? Of course, I pay her."

"No, you don't." Her words calmed dramatically, though her anger hadn't faded. "She hasn't taken a paycheck in over a year. She works for free, waiting until she could gather the courage to broach the topic of retiring."

His anger dulled, left only to be replaced by confusion and a hollowness in his chest. His gaze fell around the store only to find it drastically different than the last time he had seen it. It no longer felt like Selena's place. It smelled different. There weren't any customers. The pastries in the glass case missed her signature flare. It was all wrong. This wasn't the Moon Pie Bakery he knew.

"There hasn't been a customer since I arrived," she said softly, her voice lowering with compassion, "four hours ago."

He gasped, and his gaze snapped to hers. Everybody had loved Selena's pastries. The store used to be a hot spot around town, but it had died down when she did. He hadn't realized how dead the store had become. He was losing the store, and losing the store felt a hell of a lot like losing his wife all over again.

"Mrs. D can't keep this place open by sheer will. The rent is late." She turned around and picked up an envelope with a "Final Notice" stamp across the outside. "Neil called me when he found this. You're about to lose the store. I'm the one trying to keep it open."

Tears formed in his eyes, and he frantically tried to blink them away. Tabitha had been genuinely trying to help, but he hadn't believed that. He'd believed the worst in her. He always believed the worst. It had been a long time since he had given her the benefit of the doubt. It probably started around the time when she'd turned cold against him.

The bell over the door rang, and he turned around, filled with hope, toward the entrance, expecting a wave of customers. But the only person entering was Neil with a backpack slung over one shoulder. His jaw fell open at the sight of him, but he quickly tampered down.

"Dad?"

Bo gave his son a tight-lipped grimace, though he'd aimed for a comforting grin, and glanced back at Tabitha. Her eyes were misty and filled with a pain he knew well. He wanted to reach out, to remove the sadness he'd put there, but he couldn't. He couldn't take care of her, of anyone, not even himself. He'd failed so many times over the past three years.

But then he glanced back to his son, the boy who looked so much like Selena that it had made him weep over the years. Neil needed him. He needed his father to care for him. Bo had to step up, if not for himself, then for Neil. He had to do better, and he could start right now.

"Dinner," he said, without any sort of transition.

They both looked at him in confusion.

He faced his son. "I'm making dinner tonight. Be home by six."

A smile broke out across Neil's face. "Really?"

It had been a long time since he'd been the cause of that. It was a sight he'd sorely missed.

"Yeah, Buddy." He let a small grin come onto his face, and it felt foreign, like it didn't belong there anymore. He turned to Tabitha. She scrunched her forehead and wore a wary expression. "You'll join us, right Bis?"

She reared back, uncertain. "You want me to join you? For dinner?"

The boys shared a glance of approval, and Bo answered.

"Yes. As an apology."

A look of joy lit up her face, and he momentarily lost his breath. His gaze roamed over her hopeful eyes, the wide grin, the way she bit her lip trying to limit the smile. He'd thought he was proud to make her angry, but seeing like this, he preferred putting this expression on her face. Not many people could make her happy, and him being even a little nice had her lighting up the room. It occurred to him that he couldn't remember the last time he'd seen her so radiant. She hadn't even looked this joyful at any of her three weddings.

He glanced away, her expression too much like the sun, difficult to look at directly, and avoided her direction when he next spoke, the guilt at creating the opposite effect all those years suddenly gnawing at him. "Good, see you then."

Ducking out of the shop, Bo wondered what had happened to him and why putting a smile on Tabitha's face made him feel something just now. He couldn't pinpoint what it was exactly, but he hadn't felt something like it in years, and that terrified him.

CHAPTER 5

Tabitha followed Bo's exit with her eyes. What had come over him? He hadn't spared her any kindness in years. That wasn't them anymore. Their relationship—no, their friendship—had ended years ago. He shouldn't be inviting her to dinner, and she shouldn't be so excited to get an invitation. A niggling feeling in the pit of her stomach gave her hope they could rekindle that friendship, but she stamped down on those thoughts quickly. It did her no good to dwell on feelings like that.

They weren't the same people they once were. They'd both grown up, and they'd grown up separately. Sure, they were aware of one another through Selena, but they had gone their own ways. Their friendship hadn't evolved; it had ended. One dinner invite wasn't going to change that.

Neil tossed his backpack into a booth, cutting her contemplation short, and joined her at the counter. "What was that all about?"

She shrugged and threw an arm around his shoulder. "Dunno."

He bumped against her, and she squeezed him into her side. Though they had their scheduled Wednesday night video chats and the casual texts throughout the week, she loved having the chance to see him in person. There was nothing like having the real deal Neil in her life.

Her eyes began to mist, but she didn't want to cry in front of Neil. He didn't need another adult to care for. He was much too young for all the responsibility he'd already been given. To give her a moment to collect herself, she swept around the counter and grabbed an empty plate. "Want a snack while you study?"

"What's good today?" He said, taking a seat at the counter across from her.

Tabitha laughed darkly. "Well, Mrs. D made everything, so

you can't go wrong. I'll have to learn all her tricks before she leaves."

"Mrs. D's leaving?"

"She's retiring."

"Then who's going to..."

She watched as he glanced around worried. Placing a steady hand on the counter in front of him, she leaned forward and caught his gaze. "I am."

"What? Bis, no. I didn't call you for you to give up on your dream."

"Hey, hey, hey." She picked up a pair of tongs to grab a cookie and placed it on the plate, sliding it toward him. "Am I an adult?"

He eyed her and broke the cookie in two. "Yes," he said, holding the word for several beats.

"Then I can make my own decisions, right?" She slid around the counter and sat on the stool beside him.

"That's not what I... You have a job and a life up in New York. You can't give all of that up for me."

"I assure you I'm not." She brushed the scraggly hair off his forehead. "Yes, I came because you called, but I should have been here a long time ago. You and your dad and Saint Joshua and this bakery—you're my family, and this is my home. I shouldn't have stayed away so long. I should have been here taking care of you all."

Before Neil could argue further, the bell rang out, signaling Mrs. D's return.

"I hope y'all worked out whatever had that man's pants in a wad because, now that I've been promised retirement, I will not be coming back full-time." Mrs. D patted their shoulders as she passed.

Tabitha made a face at Neil and rolled her eyes. "I would never dream of dangling retirement in front of you only to snatch it back."

"Good," the old woman harrumphed, making her way behind the counter. She grabbed an apron and tied it around her waist. "Neil, you go do your homework. I'm fixing to teach Bis all my secrets."

Neil smirked. "You can try."

"Hey," Tabitha squealed and playfully grabbed him in a bear hug. "I'm not that hopeless in the kitchen."

The young man escaped and held his hands up in a defensive pose. "I'm just saying. How many times have you baked in the last ten years? This won't be a quick lesson, Bis."

She couldn't argue against that. Being a designer left little time for a life. When she wasn't staying at hotel rooms all over the world, she was holed up at the studio. The last time she'd cooked something other than the dinner she'd made for Neil the night before felt like eons ago. But how hard could it be to dive back into the kitchen?

***

The thing about running a bakery Tabitha hadn't considered before agreeing to take over—she wasn't a particularly good baker. Or even a mediocre baker. She could barely make toast without burning the edges. She always thought she didn't spend time in the kitchen because she didn't have the time. Now she realized she didn't make the time because she was no good.

And to keep a bakery open, you had to be good or you wouldn't have customers.

For the first time since she offered to take over the bakery,

Tabitha worried she wasn't good enough to fulfill her best friend's legacy. The muffins came out burned. The cupcakes were too dry. The frosting was runny and lumpy.

With a huff of impatience, she never realized how much work Selena had put into her treats to make everything look so effortless. The girl had had far more talent than Tabitha would ever hope to achieve with Mrs. D as a tutor. She just wasn't cut out for this, but give her a sewing machine and fabric, and she could create an original gown in no time at all.

"A little more kneading," Mrs. D said, ushering her to work the dough.

Mrs. D had moved Tabitha onto baking breads since it was unlikely she could mess that up. However, she was proving to be just as subpar as everything else she'd tried to make.

The longer it took her to make something correctly, the more frustrated she became. She left the kitchen in need of a break and sat at Neil's table to watch him study. He stuck his tongue out the side of his mouth while working out a problem, which reminded her of Selena. She'd done that all through school. Every study session, every exam.

"What're you grinning at?" Neil asked, taking a break from his math textbook and interrupting her memories.

"You look so much like your mom."

He grinned. "Really?"

"It's uncanny. I see so much of her in you, but then I see your dad, too."

He squirmed in his seat. "I'll try not to take that as an insult. I know you two don't get along."

She rested her hand on top of his and squeezed gently. "It wasn't an insult. He's a very handsome man. You should be delighted to look like him. Besides, we weren't always like this. Did you know that we grew up next door to each other?"

"Yeah?"

"Yup, we used to be great friends. We would talk through our windows and play together outside and point out constellations together. We were really close." She thought about all the games they'd played growing up, how close they were, how much time she spent with him. They would play in his treehouse and lay under the stars, and he'd even taught her how to throw a football. Other than Selena, Bo was her best friend growing up, at least until high school. She'd known things had had to change, but she never would have thought they'd change so much.

"What ended it?"

Her vision grew cloudy as she thought back to why things changed. The only answer she could come up with was a dance their junior year. That night had changed a lot, not just between her and Bo and then between Bo and Selena, but it also changed her relationship with Selena irrevocably. No matter how hard she tried to pretend it hadn't, she couldn't deny it.

"It doesn't matter. It's in the past." She gave him a sad smile.

"Bis," he said, his voice cracking. "Whatever he did, he's an idiot."

Tabitha chuckled and patted his hand. "What makes you think he did something wrong?"

"Didn't he?"

Neil assumed his father was to blame, and on one hand, he was. But also not. Things happened. Life changed. Nothing stayed the same forever. As much as it was his fault, it was also Tabitha's fault. And Selena's fault. There was enough blame to go around, but also Tabitha couldn't blame anybody. It was just the luck of the draw.

Her lips parted to argue, but she couldn't make them form the words. It was a difficult situation to explain, especially to teenager, but most especially to the teenage son of the two other members of this weird scenario.

"I knew it." He groaned and looked down at his work. "I'm sorry for whatever he did. I wonder how different things would have been if you'd never stopped being friends, if he never..."

The door opened, knocking into the bell hanging above it, and Neil's words fell away. Two girls around his age walked into the bakery. After ordering from Mrs. D, they sat in the corner by the front window. One girl glanced over at him and smiled. Neil's cheeks flamed, and Tabitha fought a grin at the sight.

Neil had a crush.

She was excited to be able to witness the moment. She missed so much over the years that getting this moment was magical. Seeing his first crush, the innocence of first love, was adorable and terrifying and made her feel old and also worried that she'd mess it up for him somehow. But, she was here. And that had to be a good first step in helping him navigate this stage of life.

She clucked her tongue to get his attention, and his gaze snapped to hers.

"What?" his voice cracked again. When Neil finished puberty, he would be a force to be reckoned with, especially if he was already catching the eye of girls as pretty as this one.

"You should ask her out." She smirked knowingly.

"Who?"

"Who?" She scoffed and dramatically threw her hands up. "That pretty girl over there who can't keep her eyes off of you, and who you've been watching since she walked in."

"No, no... I can't. She's way out of my league." He cleared his throat and pretended to focus on his homework, but his eyes returned to the pretty girl in the corner.

Tabitha glanced between the two young adults while sliding out of the booth and tutted at him. "I don't think she feels that way."

CHAPTER 6

Thoughts of the bakery assaulted Bo's mind his entire journey home. He couldn't believe he'd let things get as bad as they were. Mrs. D hadn't been taking a paycheck but kept everything running so he didn't have to worry about it. He loved the old woman, like a second mother, but that was unacceptable. He needed to let her go and find a permanent replacement if he wanted to keep the bakery open.

He paused, stopping short in the middle of the hallway. He didn't want to close the bakery, but there might not be another option. Who wanted to right the ship on a failing bakery? He couldn't guarantee that anyone who came in now to help would even have a job in a few months' time.

Glenn was right. Tabitha couldn't take it over. She needed to live her life. And be happy. That's all he wanted for her. A perfectly content smile gracing her face. She hadn't had that in a long time, and he realized he'd missed it. They were so close growing up; playing together in the yard that extended between the front of their houses; having a handmade telephone line hanging between their bedroom windows and talking late into the night, well past bedtime; her dancing like an idiot to Backstreet Boys when she thought she was all alone.

That smile had been absent, however, over the years. He hated each of her husbands. Not one of them had been able to put it on her face. He never understood how she could get married three times and not once look happy about it, look beyond ecstatic to join her soul to the love of her life. She was a beautiful, intelligent woman who could have any guy she wanted. So why did she always pick guys who made her look miserable? Who couldn't be bothered to make the small amount of effort needed to induce a smile like that? Just a bit of kindness from him did it. How could they fail so spectacularly?

He entered the kitchen and opened the fridge but closed

it when the cell phone from inside his pocket rang. His agent's name popped up on the caller ID. He stared at the screen in front of him, contemplating ignoring it, but wanted to get this call over with. It would be a fair bit of chastisement. The longer he put it off, the worse it would become.

"Schuyler," he answered shortly.

"How's the story coming?" She never had time—or care—for pleasantries, and he tended to appreciate that about her.

But not today. Today he wanted to keep her talking long enough to come up with something he could use to bullshit his way out of the conversation. No such luck.

From the pregnant pause, she must have realized he still didn't have a plot. Or characters. Or setting. Or a basic idea from which to sprout any of those things.

"How is Tabitha?"

"Fine," he answered, his feathers rankling. He knew she had reason to bring her up but couldn't think of one. They got along, much to his dismay, but hadn't seen each other in years... as far as he knew. Though, he conceded, they both lived in New York. They might very well have met up without telling him.

"You don't sound like you want to kill her anymore."

"No, we're finding... a common ground, I guess, though it's been tense."

"You could always use that tension as inspiration," she said, a strange knowing lilt coloring her words that made him instantly suspicious.

"What do you mean?"

"Write a fight scene between your two main characters, use some of the tension that exists between you and Tabitha as inspiration. With how much you two bicker, you'd have half a story right there. All you have to do then is write the falling in love part."

Bo's blood ran cold. He didn't want to think about Tabitha in that way. Even if he wasn't the one who would be looking at her through a romantic lens, his character would be. He'd always written with Selena on his mind, but he wouldn't be able to do that if he had to think about Tabitha.

"No."

"Come on, Gallagher. The enemies-to-lovers trope sells, yet you've never used it."

"It's been done. A lot."

"Yes, by Shakespeare and Austen... Even Joss Whedon on Buffy. Twice actually—Cordelia and Xander, then again with Buffy and Spike. You know that certain tropes never go out of style. They keep selling and selling, and oh! You know who else has used it? My personal favorite—I'm sure you know of him— Nicholas Sparks. Now that I think of it, you're right. If Nicholas Sparks does it, I'm not sure you'd be able to do it any justice."

That sent a shot of anger through him. Nicholas freaking Sparks. He was the bane of Bo's existence. Everything Bo wrote was always compared to and found lacking against a Sparks novel. He had never read his competitor's books, but everything he wrote looked like the idea was borrowed from his predecessor.

"You really think that'll work on me? I see what you're doing."

"I wasn't being subtle."

He barked a laugh.

"Think about it. You haven't been able to write on your own. Try writing the beginning, using you and Tabitha, a bitter battle between two old foes. That I know you can do. She's wanted to strangle you for as long as I've known her. You won't struggle for ideas. And, you never know, a story might come to you as you put pen to page."

That's what he was afraid of. He always wrote from a place of truth, but he couldn't do that from a place of truth about Tabitha. The idea of using her as romantic inspiration made him uneasy and left him feeling just a little bit guilty. He didn't want to think of anyone but Selena in that way. She was the love of his life. Forever and always.

"You're on the clock, Gallagher. If you can't write a story, you owe the publisher. A lot, I might add. You don't have to mean the words or feel what this character feels. You don't have to have them come to life like that. Just put words down and tell a story. Make something up. We can flesh it out together." The sound of her fingers snapping came through the line. "I got it! Pretend you're telling Tabitha's future kids the story of how she fell in love. Make it the most fantastical plot you've ever written. If you're going to quit, let's go out on a bang."

Though she kept talking, his brain cancelled out the words. He was too focused on the idea of Tabitha's future children. It angered him more than it should, leaving him with more confusion and anger than he could explain having. He didn't wish ill on her, not at all, but thinking of her having children, having a life with someone, sounded wrong. Sure, she'd been married before, but Bo never believed any of those relationships would actually last. He could see how wrong each of them was for her. Her husbands were more friend than husband. Instead of figuring out why the thought upset him, he quickly ended the call with his agent and cleared through the papers on the kitchen counter.

Envelope after envelope had piled up, each one waiting for him to work his way through the pile. After creating two stacks— one for all the junk mail and a much shorter one for legitimate business—he found a postcard dated almost a year ago. It was a reminder from the dentist that Neil needed to come in for his bi-annual cleaning.

Bo leaned onto the counter and groaned, chastising himself for falling so far into his own world. He had let his son fall through the cracks, and he hated himself for it. Needing to take a small step in the right direction, he grabbed his phone and made an appointment for the following day. He apologized to the receptionist for the oversight and promised a more consistent treatment going forward.

When that was complete, he felt better. It was a trivial accomplishment, but one he had needed to take. He glanced around the kitchen and pondered what to make for dinner, especially after making such a big deal about it by inviting Tabitha. He knew he'd need to make a grocery run since he couldn't remember the last time he'd filled the cabinets. His culinary skills were limited, but there was one dish he could make after growing up in the South—jambalaya. Nobody made it better than him. Well, okay, probably lots of people could make it better than him, but his was damned good.

He wrote a list of the ingredients he'd need, adding a few staple items and treats he guessed Neil hadn't had a long time, the first steps to making up for lost time. He wanted to show Neil, Tabitha, and himself he could take care of everyone.

The first step was dinner.

Chapter 7

Tabitha was pleasantly surprised when she walked into the Gallagher house that evening and a delicious scent greeted her. She wound her way into the kitchen. Bo was standing at the stove while Neil set the table with three place settings. The sight surprised her so much, she couldn't move. It all felt so domestic, so... not what she'd been expecting. How had Bo changed his perspective around so quickly?

As her eyes roamed over Bo's form, an impressed grin grew across her face. He was dressed. Not that he hadn't been covered the times she'd seen since she came home, but he had replaced the sweats and t-shirts that had been his staples. He wore a simple gray polo shirt that curved with his arms and sleek black slacks that just a might too tight in the bum, but she wasn't going to complain. Since she couldn't have him, the next best thing was to enjoy the view, and the simple act of cleaning up made her giddy. Maybe he really would start to move on and care for his son and house again. She wouldn't have to worry so much when she returned to New York.

Her smile fell away.

"If you stare for much longer, you're going to make me self-conscious," Bo teased, smirking over his shoulder at her.

She blinked and turned to Neil, silently asking the questions on her mind. He shrugged but could barely contain his grin. He was delighted to get his father back, and she couldn't fault him for that.

"Smells good," she murmured, rubbing her hand over Neil's hair before taking a seat at the table.

"Thanks," Bo said, his voice quiet, timid.

Neil beamed over the table. "I helped."

"I'm glad. You'll need to learn how to make things other than ramen and peanut butter and jelly sandwiches when you go off to college. It's good you're starting early."

Bo winced. His pained expression was a sharp stab to Tabitha's gut. She hadn't realized how upsetting the thought of Neil going to college might have been, but clearly the impending departure of his last remaining family member worried him.

"Dinner's ready," Bo said, changing the subject and carrying a pot of food to the table. "Oh, and Neil, I made you a dentist appointment for tomorrow. You haven't gone in a while." He gave an embarrassed shrug as he set the food on the potholder in the center of the table.

Though it smelled delicious and full of spicy flavor, the sight of it almost made Tabitha lose her appetite. She glanced up and caught Neil's gaze.

"I take it back," he grinned. "I didn't help with that."

"Yuck it up," Bo huffed, smacking Neil with a dish towel. "Bis, can you serve while I grab the biscuits?"

"You made biscuits, too?" She was terrified, until he admitted they were already made. He just baked them until they turned golden brown. "Thank god! You're nowhere near ready to conquer good, Southern biscuits."

Neil chuckled behind his glass of water.

When Bo joined them, Tabitha waited for him to eat the brown, lumpy concoction before giving it a try herself. When he didn't keel over or express any disgust, she considered it was safe enough. When she took a small bite, the taste was far better than she expected. It might have looked disgusting, but that was the only downside she found.

"Mmm..." she moaned. "What is this?"

She looked up to find Bo watching her with a pained expression.

"Do I have something on my face?"

"No, you just... uh... you reminded me of someone for a second."

Tabitha met Neil's gaze, but he had a grin covering his face. "Mom used to do that all the time."

"Oh," she said, turning back to Bo. "Sorry."

"Don't be." He still looked pained, but he waved off her apology. "Sometimes you can't help but remember."

Wasn't that the truth? At random times, the pain of that loss overtook her too, especially when she did something her best friend loved, like spending time in a kitchen or taking care of

Neil. It was those things that made her feel close to Selena again. Doing them made her smile, not cry, though she never ended up baking anything remotely as good as her friend. Or until she even came back home. She should bake more often after she went home, though she couldn't bring any of it to work. The models would turn up their noses, and the designers would laugh her right out of the studio for being so domestic. It really was a rat race at the top.

Neil sent pleading eyes in her direction. "Bis, you think you could give me some girl advice?"

The topic shift caused the pain on Bo's face to disappear, replaced by a smirk of mischievousness. "Oh? Who's the lucky girl to have captured your attention?"

"I don't want to say," Neil answered carefully, giving an awkward sideways glance toward his father.

Tabitha suspected she knew who the girl was but didn't want to out the young man if he wasn't ready to own up to his feelings. As much as she wanted to help him, though, she was probably horrible at giving love advice. She drank down half her glass of water, wishing it was a glass of wine. "I'm not the person to ask."

"Yeah, why would you go to her for love advice? She's been divorced, how many times now? Like seven?"

A silence descended across the room. The comment smarted, and it felt like a blow to her heart. She knew her three failed marriages was a high number, but she couldn't make herself feel anything that wasn't there, not when her heart had been given away a long time ago. But at least she tried, giving what she could to her marriages, until it was no longer enough for her husbands. The best part about her divorces, though, was none of her exes were upset or angry with her. Although their relationships didn't work out, she maintained great friendships with all of them that continued long after the ink was dry on the divorce papers. Though Henry, her third husband, had been distancing himself from her since he'd started dating his current girlfriend. She expected he'd be proposing to her any day now, and it made sense not to maintain a friendship with his ex-wife in that regard.

A confused expression spread across Bo's face as he took in the sight of his son, who was white-knuckling his fork, and Tabitha fighting back the moisture forming in her eyes.

"That was rude," she said, as calm as she could be.

"What? I'm only teasing."

"You know that thing mom used to say?" Neil asked through gritted teeth. He had always been protective of Tabitha, which filled her heart and took away some of the pain of Bo's remark. "If you can't say anything nice, don't say anything at all."

Bo was taken aback at how Neil had spoken to him. He met Tabitha's gaze, his face crumpling when he saw her pain. "I'm sorry, Bis. I didn't mean to hurt you."

Tabitha pasted on a fake smile, one she reserved for moments specifically spent in Bo's company over the years and shrugged. "No worries. It's true, right? I'm The Divorcee. God, that sounds like a bad superhero."

"That's not what I m—"

"So, about this girl?" she turned to Neil, cutting his father off and changing the subject.

Neil glared at his father for a few seconds longer before refocusing on Tabitha. "Well, I guess the big question is... how do I get her to like me?"

"That I really don't know!" Tabitha barked on a humorless laugh. "The only guy I've ever loved never loved me in return."

"How's that possible? You were married three times!" Bo said.

The fact he knew the correct number only made her angrier. He didn't have to exaggerate it earlier. She stared him right in the eye and spoke calmly. "Sure, I loved them. Still do. But I've never been in love with any of them. I've never been able to get over my first love. It's sad really, quite pathetic."

"Who was it?" Bo asked. "Do I know him? Did we go to school together?"

She shook her head, knowing she'd never answer those questions. She couldn't. She'd kept that a secret for years, not even Selena knew, and she'd be damned if she'd let it spill now.

"Come on, Bis. Just tell us," Neil whined. "It's not like I'd know who it was anyway."

"No." She took a bite of her food and tried to steer the conversation away. "If you want to know how to convince someone to go out with you, you should ask your father. Selena couldn't stand him when we were kids."

"Uh un, no changing the subject. You're telling us who this perfect first love is," Bo demanded. "Was it Tommy Mercer? God, I always hated that guy. I can't believe you ended up dating him after he harassed you like that."

"Was it Uncle Glenn? You two always looked so chummy together."

"I know." Bo snapped his fingers at her. "Was it the history teacher? You know, what's his name? There were all those rumors that you secretly dated him."

"Stop," she said, shoving a harsh finger in Bo's face. "I never dated any of our teachers, and you damn well know that."

"Just tell us who it was, and we'll stop. Right, dad?"

"Of course." Mischievousness sparkled in Bo's eyes. "We promise."

"No. Let's get back to—"

"Please, please, please?"

"No. The girl from—"

"Please, please, please!" Neil's begging became more incessant and louder.

"Neil, please stop—"

"Please, Bis. Please, please, please."

Tabitha couldn't take it anymore. The words burst from her mouth before she could restrain herself. "Fine! He never loved me because he was in love with my best friend!" She gasped the moment the words left her lips, as if she could recall them from being heard. Her eyes grew wide, and she dropped her gaze to her plate. "I am so, so sorry. This is why I didn't want to say."

A clank across the table brought her gaze to Neil. He had dropped his fork onto his plate. She couldn't tell what expression was on his face—hurt, shock, confusion. It was understandable. Nobody ought to hear that someone who was practically their aunt was in love with their father. It was a messed-up situation, which was why Tabitha had to leave all those years ago. She could no longer take seeing him so happy with someone else, even if that someone was her best friend in the world.

"Neil—" she began, but her words were cut off when he abruptly stood, his chair scratching against the floor in his escape.

He ran from the room, and she heard the slamming of his door not a minute later.

"He's going to hate me," she said, a tear slipping down her cheek.

"No, he's not. He's confused, and I can't say I blame him."

Bo's voice was gruff, and she was afraid to meet his gaze. Instead, she stared at where her favorite person disappeared down the hallway.

"Why didn't you ever tell me?" He sounded pained, like this announcement hurt him.

That's when she met his gaze. She was the one who had suffered, who spent years with heartache, who had to keep the secret from her best friend. He could stuff it. "When would I have done that, Bo? When you chose my best friend at winter formal? When you said your wedding vows? Or at the hospital when Neil was born? Tell me when would have been a suitable time to tell you? Because I've been wracking my brain for damn near twenty-five years, and I still don't think you should have ever found out!"

"Bis, I get that it's bad... timing, or whatever, but I deserve to know, don't you think? I mean, damn!"

She huffed out her frustration and stood, taking her plate into the kitchen. She dumped the food into the trash and placed the plate in the dishwasher. He followed her but had to complete an about face when she stormed forward with purpose, heading for the front door. Stuffing her arms into her jacket and slipping her purse onto her shoulder, she finally spoke. "I'll take Neil to his dentist appointment tomorrow. He and I need to talk. I need to explain. I can't have him hate me."

"That's fine, but you know we have to talk, too, Bis. You owe me that much."

All the repressed anger over the last twenty years—since the night he and Selena got together—came up all at once. "I don't owe you jack," she spat and slipped out the door.

After slamming it closed behind her, she leaned on it as quietly as she could and sighed. She was about to lose the only things she ever really cared about, and she didn't know how to fix it. She hoped Neil would let her explain before cutting her off for good, but she couldn't blame him if that was his decision.

Chapter 8

Hoping his tangled feelings would become clear through his work, Bo sat down to write. He did what Schuyler recommended, but after he'd set up two characters in a fight that ended in a very angry—though extremely passionate—sex scene, his feelings were more jumbled than before. His characters had developed minds of their own, and no matter how much he tried putting them back in their boxes, they also fought him every step of the way.

Then, when he knocked on Neil's door, he was met with a harsh cry to be left alone.

Neil didn't want to talk. Tabitha didn't want to talk. Well, Bo wanted to talk dammit, and his characters didn't seem to want to listen.

God, he needed a beer.

He pulled out his phone and called up his sister. Not because he was anxious to talk to her about the bombshell Tabitha left behind, but because he wanted someone at the house while he went out. Neil didn't need a babysitter, but maybe he'd talk to his Aunt Bethany.

"This can't possibly be my big brother who never calls me," her voice trilled into the phone when she answered. "I'm pretty sure he doesn't even know I exist."

A new wave of guilt flushed through him. He needed to do better about making sure the people he loved knew they were loved.

"Yeah, sorry... I'm a jerk."

"I'm pretty used to you by now."

Bo rolled his eyes. His sister was too much sometimes. "Are you busy right now? I need someone to look after Neil for a bit."

"What's happened?" Her tone was flint.

Bo sighed. He wanted to talk about what Bis said, but not to his baby sister. He'd rather eat a whole colony of bees or, heaven forbid, help his grandmother out of the bath.

"It's nothing serious, but he just got some news and won't talk to me about it. I hoped he'd talk to someone who wasn't his father."

"Fair." She clucked her tongue in thought, something she'd done since they were kids. "You going to tell me so I can prepare myself?"

The pain in Tabitha's eyes flashed through his mind. Telling his sister felt like gossiping, and he wouldn't do that to Bis. If she wanted Beth to know, she would have told her.

"No. If he wants to tell you, that's his business. But I don't feel comfortable being the one to say it."

She growled. "Fine. I'll be right over."

"Thanks. I'm going to nip over to the Schuh Factory with Glenn... Maybe bring some ice cream with you. It might help get him to open up."

While waiting for his sister to arrive, he texted Glenn to meet him and paced up and down the first-floor hallway. Had he really been so blind all these years? Had Selena? Why did Bis say something now? Surely, she couldn't be in love with him. She was mistaken. They didn't know anything about each other anymore. Okay, so he knew she lived in New York and worked for Antonio Riviera, that famous fashion mogul, but that was general knowledge. Her parents still lived here, and word spreads around town like a virus. Especially in one as small as St. Joshua. And alright, maybe he knew her designs made it into Antonio's fashion shows this season. It wasn't like he stalked her. Schuyler was obsessed with her work and mentioned anytime Bis had found some success. He couldn't very well stop his agent from giving him news.

Bo's feet stopped, and his head popped up, alert. Was this why she moved away? Was this why she stayed away? Was he responsible for the distance between his wife and her best friend?

The door opened, slamming into the wall. His sister stumbled inside, a stuffed paper bag from the grocery store weighing her down.

"Alright there?" he asked.

Bethany blew her bangs from her face and readjusted the bag. "Fine, yeah, why? Don't I look fine?"

"You look like a twig ready to snap." Bo stepped forward and swiped the bag from her hands. With a glance inside to the ice cream and marshmallows and potato chips and other junk foods, he raised his eyebrow at her.

"What?" she asked innocently. "The way to a growing boy's heart is junk food. And when he's stuffing food in, he can't help but let the words out."

He shook his head and turned toward the kitchen, suppressing a grin along the way. She really did nail the male psyche.

***

When he arrived at the Schuh Factory, the family-owned bar not far from his house, Bo removed his leather jacket and hung it off the back of his bar stool. He gestured to the bartender, Phil, for a beer and sat beside his best friend. He rubbed his hands over his face and sighed. Everything was slipping from his grip—Selena, the bakery, Neil... even Bis.

Phil slid a beer across the bar, and Bo chugged half of it down before taking a breath.

"You alright?" Glenn asked. He sipped from his own IPA and waited with raised eyebrows.

Bo took a sip. He didn't know how to put words to everything that evening. Even he had trouble believing it. He couldn't think of a time when Tabitha would have had feelings for him. It just didn't seem real.

"Can I ask you a question?" he said to Glenn. "Have you ever been blindsided by something and not known how you felt about it? Like, everything you thought you knew turned out to be backward?"

Glenn took a long drag from his bottle and sighed. "You mean Bis's feelings for you?"

Bo's gaze shot to his friend's face. "You knew?"

"Man, anyone who wasn't blind saw how that girl felt about you." He paused for a drink and tilted the beer in Bo's direction. "You remember that time Tommy Mercer bullied her to get her to agree to a date? And you put a stop to it? I'm pretty sure that's when it all started. You were like her knight in shining armor after that. Who knows? It could have gone on for even longer, but that's when I noticed it."

"I hated that guy." Bo frowned into his mug.

"So did she. Bis only dated him after that to get a response out of you. She kept on dating him because she hoped you'd get so jealous that you'd eventually ask her out yourself." Glenn drank from his beer. He looked at his friend with a worried glance, unsure if he should continue. "You remember that night you realized you had feelings for Selena?"

Bo nodded and a small smile appeared. A dreamy expression crossed his face at the memory. In the middle of the winter formal, surrounded by a sea of people, Selena danced alone like she was the only person in the room. He felt such a strong yearning for her, one he'd never experienced before. She'd awoken something in him that died the day she did. "Like it was yesterday. She always danced like no one was watching."

"Well, I remember it a different way, I'm sure. As does Bis." Glenn rubbed his hand over his buzz cut. "You and I, we both went stag, and you'd been complaining you were bored, so I suggested you ask someone to dance, specifically someone like Tabitha. You said some bullshit about knowing her all your life and her not being your type and just being friends and blah blah. What you didn't know... she was right behind you at the time. Dude, you should have seen how crushed she was. Heartbroken, that girl."

"What does that have to do with Selena?" He pulled his eyebrows together and turned to face Glenn more fully.

"That magical moment when you watched Selena dance to Fly Me to the Moon... Yeah, that was Selena dancing like an idiot to Tabitha's favorite song and trying to get Tabitha to dance with her to make Tabitha feel better about not being asked to dance. Selena only danced like that because she was trying to cheer up her best friend."

Glenn enunciated Tabitha's name each time he said it, like a hammer pounding a nail, each strike driving deeper into Bo's chest. God, he was such a heel.

"Apparently, Selena hated that song until you two started dating and learned you liked it. The reason you were hit with feelings that night was actually because of the girl who 'wasn't your type.' It's always been Tabitha's favorite... I mean it was... that is until you two danced to it at your wedding. Oh, man... You should have seen her that night. She was in a right state."

Glenn blew out a harsh breath, and his eyes bulged from the memory.

"Is that why she disappeared? Selena was crushed when she couldn't find her." Bo remembered how stressed his bride had been because she couldn't find her maid of honor. Tabitha had disappeared after the toasts, along with the best man. Bo had assumed they'd hooked up because of the magic of the wedding and the free-flowing booze. He hadn't even considered she disappeared for any other reason.

"Think for a second how hurt Tabitha must have felt, watching you marry her best friend and not being able to say a freaking word." Glenn shook his head. "I took care of her as she drunkenly bawled her eyes out about it. Man, I never knew you were worth so many tears."

Pain sliced through his gut, and his stomach filled with dread. He never wanted to be the cause of heartache. But then a thought occurred to him that threatened everything he knew. "Did she know about it? Selena?"

"Don't think so. Bis never said a word about if she did or not. But everyone else who weren't the two of you knew. Everyone else saw." Glenn gestured around the bar, as if the other patrons were all part of their conversation. "That girl... this woman... she's a far better person than any of us."

"How so?"

Glenn turned in his seat and stared at him, like Bo was the densest person alive. And after Bis's admission, he felt like it.

"She kept her mouth shut, suffered in silence, so that the two people she loved most in the world could be happy together, even if it meant she would be forever miserable. Is there any doubt in your mind that, had Bis said anything to Selena, you two wouldn't've broken up? Of course, you would have, because Selena loved her like a goddamn sister. And Bis knew that. All she had to do was tell Selena about her feelings, and you two would have been done, finito, but she didn't, and she's doing it all over again."

He knew Glenn was right. Selena was just as selfless and would have given up the world if it could make Tabitha happy. They were the same in that way.

"What's she doing now?"

"She's giving up her own happiness for you and your family, you moron. She's risking her career—her life—up in New York, for what? So, she can have you? No, because she doesn't believe she has a chance with you, especially not after all this time. Because it's easy to come down here, take your wrath, and save a business she never had any ambition to run? Don't think so. To take care of your kid after years of hoping she'd have one with you? Not a chance in hell, though she loves Neil with all her heart... She did it because Tabitha Grace McElmore is the most selfless, caring person in the world and is willing to give up her own happiness and stability for those she loves, which includes you, you shithead. You'd be a selfish dumbass if you let her stay."

"What am I supposed to do, kick her out? She's not staying with me. Tell her to go home? I have, and she didn't listen. Tell her it's never going to hap—"

"Yes," Glenn said, looking him straight in the eye, "if that's the truth."

Bo balked. For some reason, he couldn't imagine her leaving. Not now. Not anymore. Saint Joshua felt more like home now that she was back than it had in a long time.

"If you can't love that girl the way she deserves, if you can't move forward and fall in love and find happiness with her, tell her to leave. She doesn't need to hope for something that'll only break her heart again when it doesn't happen. But if you can, if you can love her, genuinely, genuinely love her and not just how she reminds you of Selena, then find a way to make her happy. She deserves it."

He snorted. "Please, even if... if I could... even if I did have feelings for her, she'd never move back here permanently." His words made him angry, but he couldn't pinpoint the reason. More than that, he wasn't sure he wanted to figure it out.

"Do you remember what her dream was when we were kids? Her all-time, lifelong goal?" Glenn pulled out his wallet and slapped a twenty onto the bar, making sure to make eye contact with Phil. "All she ever wanted was to have her own boutique right here in town. She and Selena were going to be shop neighbors and hang out together every day, and she could create her own designs from her own studio. She would happily move home if she thought she had even a chance with you."

Glenn gave him a knowing look as he put on his coat, and Bo rubbed his eyes with his palms, uncertain how to proceed with this knowledge.

"If you can see yourself with her, all you need to do is let her know. But if not, end it before you hurt that woman even more."

With those final words, Glenn left him to think about how everything he thought he'd ever known was wrong.

CHAPTER 9

Tabitha sat in the school office, waiting for Neil to arrive from class. She couldn't wait much longer to talk to him, hating that he was mad at her. In his thirteen years, they'd never fought, never been angry. They had developed a close friendship, as close as an adult woman can be with a teenage boy without being creepy. To be fair, she knew more about Neil than Neil knew about her. She didn't feel comfortable telling him nearly as much as Selena or even Bo knew about her.

Neil meandered into the office but froze when he saw her sitting there. He swallowed hard and stared at his feet.

Dread flowed through her, but she stood and crossed the small room, laying a comforting hand on his shoulder. A hooded expression crossed his face, and she took her hand back. His reaction left a crack in her heart. This was why she'd never said a word. She couldn't bear losing everyone she ever loved. And despite everything, despite him being someone else's child to a man she'd always loved, Tabitha loved Neil with all her heart. She was there the day he was born, the day he learned to walk and speak. He was the closest thing she'd ever have to a child of her own, and she could feel him slipping through her fingers.

"Ready?" she asked, voice cracking.

He nodded and left through the exit without her.

When she caught up to him, Neil was leaning against the passenger door of her rental car with an earbud in each ear. She prayed their talk would be like all their other conversations—light, breezy, easy—but she knew that was too much to hope for. She only prayed he would at least hear her out instead of shutting her out of his life for good.

She crawled behind the wheel and started the car. After she turned onto the main road, she yanked the earbud from his ear facing her. He looked her way in surprise and caught her eye.

"Much better," she said. "We need to talk."

"Don't say it. I already know."

"What is it that you think you know?"

"I know you hate me."

His voice was meek and cracked halfway through, and his words shattered her heart the rest of the way. She pulled off the road, cutting in front of an angry driver in the process, and slammed the gear into park. Turning in her seat to give him her full attention, she cupped his chin and raised it enough so he couldn't help but look her square in the eye. His eyes were glossy, pained, close to spilling over.

"Neil—Little Bit—I could never hate you... ever." She willed him to hear the honesty in her words. "Your mom, she was my best friend. Hell, we were closer than that. She was my sister, and you were the absolute world to that girl, which means you are the absolute world to me. How I felt—about your dad will never change the fact I will always, always love you. Nothing, and I mean nothing, will ever stop that. You hear me?"

A tear slipped down his face, and he folded his lips between his teeth as he nodded.

"I need you to say it. I need to hear that you know beyond

any shadow of a doubt that I am always here for you. You call me, and I will come running. I will drop everything there is in this world if you need anything, and I mean it!"

"I know, Bis."

Pulling him forward, she wrapped her arms around him and held on. She wanted there to be no doubt in his mind that he was her world. She would die before he questioned his worth to her again. His hands gripped her like she was his lifeline.

Their relationship was safe. Her heart starting repairing itself, but she still had one more conversation that might fracture it some more.

"Can I ask you something," he said, his words and tears seeping into her shoulder.

"Anything, always, forever, Little Bit."

Neil leaned back, and Tabitha let her hands fall from the embrace.

"Do you still love him?"

A gasp slipped through her lips before she could hold it back. Looking into his eyes, she considered her answer before speaking. He needed to know the truth if she wanted any hope of keeping his trust, and she needed to keep his trust if she had any hope of keeping him in her life. She needed him. Not just because he was her best friend's son, but because he made her feel again. She was always so proud of him when he won a game and was so happy when he reached out to her for advice. She felt like a person because of him, not like the robot she was at work or in the city.

Tabitha nodded. "I've never stopped loving your dad."

A grin spread across his face, and his eyes lit with excitement. That expression meant trouble. "So then..."

"No."

"You don't even know what I was going to say."

"Yes, I do—it's written all over your face—and the answer is no."

"But he's different when you're around. I can see it."

Tabitha sighed and leaned back into her seat. "Bo... he's... he'll be in love with your mom until the day he dies. She was it for him. Even I could see it. That's probably why it hurt so much... because even I knew they were soulmates." She stared out the window at the cars driving past, reliving painful memories. Swallowing them down, she pointed a finger at him. "I don't want you scheming. You got it? Leave that man alone."

"You guys could be happy together."

"No, we couldn't." Tabitha turned away and thought of his wedding. She knew in her gut he would never look at her the way his eyes sparkled as Selena walked down the aisle. "He'd grow to resent me because I'm not her, and I would resent him because he'd never be able to love me, not like he loved her... You know, kid, not everyone gets their happily ever after."

Neil slammed his fist against the dash and growled. "Dammit, Bis!"

"Hey, hey, hey... Language!"

"Sorry, but I want you to be happy. You do everything for everybody else. You should do what you can to make you happy."

"I..." Tabitha didn't know what to say, but she didn't have time to come up with a response. She thanked the high heaven when her cellphone rang but decided it was a lateral move when the name appeared on the screen. "Hello."

"Thank god you're alive," Bo said frantically.

"Of course, we are. What's going on?"

"I got a call from Neil's dentist asking if he was still coming. Care to explain?"

She grabbed Neil's hand and smiled. "We were clearing the air. We're heading there now."

When his voice returned, it had a note of concern. "Everything all right?"

"We worked it out."

"Good." He was quiet for a moment. "Listen, Bis, you think you could come by after you drop him off at soccer practice? I think we should talk."

"Bo..." She sighed and rubbed her forehead.

"Please?"

And since Tabitha was never any good at denying the Gallagher men a thing, especially when they said the magic word, she agreed. "Fine, but we are not talking about that."

"Oh, yes... yes, we are." His voice lowered, all stern like, and it sent a chill through her.

She hung up the phone and looked over to the young man beside her. "Sometimes I hate that man."

"No, you don't," he said with a teasing, all-knowing grin.

"No, I don't. But that doesn't mean I like him very much right now." She moved the gearshift into drive and pulled back onto the road. "Let's get you to your cleaning before he calls me again."

"Like that'd be a bad thing," Neil joked with a smirk.

Tabitha chuckled but realized it really wouldn't be. Especially if he could love her, like Neil thought was possible. She shook that thought right out of her head. Neil was trying to plant the seeds of an impossible future in her head. Which was ridiculous. She should be the one teasing him about crushes and unrequited feelings. How had the tables gotten so turned around? She would have to think of a way to get rid of that smirk before he thought of a way to intervene. He did not need to get caught up in the middle of this. Tabitha had realized many moons ago she could never have the happily ever after with Bo. It was not in the stars for them, and if Neil schemed and failed, it would break his heart. And beat up heart was enough for the two of them.

***

After the dentist appointment where no less than two cavities were found, Tabitha dropped Neil off at his soccer practice. Needing some armor before talking with Bo, she swung by her parents' house to change her outfit. She pulled into the driveway as her father was getting out of his pickup truck.

"Hi, honey," he said, crossing to her, kissing her on the cheek, and leading her toward the front door. "How's Neil doing?"

"He's good. I just took him to soccer."

"Any plans for the night?" he asked, opening the front door. "Honey, I'm home!" he shouted to her mom inside.

"Yeah, I'm changing quickly and going to talk with Bo."

"Really? I guess we won't wait up then." Her father gave her a cheeky grin, and she smacked his arm in response.

"Not you, too!"

Her mother strode into the room with her needle point. "What's your father doing now?"

"What do you mean me, too?"

Tabitha sighed and looked from her father to her mother then down at the ground. She needed to tell them. They both knew the real reason she moved to New York all those years ago was because it hurt her too much to see Bo with Selena. It got harder to bear the longer she had to witness it. Moving away had been her mother's suggestion, and at first, Tabitha was against it. Then the idea rooted in her mind until she didn't have another option.

"I accidentally let it spill at dinner last night that I'd had feelings for Bo."

Her mother's gasp felt a little over the top, but her dad's chuckle was damned annoying.

"I knew it would come out eventually," her dad said, groaning as he settled into his chair. "How's Neil feel about it?"

Her mother led her to the sofa, and they both took a seat. Like a pro, she studiously stared at the magazine covers spread haphazardly on the coffee table instead of meeting her mother's all-seeing gaze.

"He's fine. We worked it out." She paused. "And I'm talking with Bo tonight."

"Oh, well, that man wouldn't recognize a good thing if it bonked him over the head. Speaking of which, you should bonk him over the head," her mother teased, turning her attention to her needle point.

"Good luck, honey," her father said before turning on the television. "If you need us later, try to only wake your mother. I need my beauty sleep."

"Geez, I'm really feeling the love right now," she said, crossing the living room for the stairs.

"I don't know why," her father said with a hearty laugh. "That'll come tonight."

CHAPTER 10

Bo was focused on his computer, rewriting the scene that had devolved so quickly the day before. His characters wanted to have sex more than he wanted to finish the book. His ambition and inspiration were running on fumes. To try getting his characters to slow down getting together, he decided to write them as friends and take out the whole enemies-to-lovers trope. There was a fine line between love and hate, after all, and he wanted to stop the creeping thought of Tabitha while thinking of his characters and what the choices they kept repeating on the page.

He took his hands off the keys of his computer, wondering when he had started thinking of Tabitha as his enemy and couldn't pinpoint a time he ever had. They were friends as kids, and then she stopped talking to him. Even when she was giving him the silent treatment, he never thought of her as his enemy, so why was he likening her to his male protagonist's enemy? She was always too pure for that, for someone in need of an archnemesis. Even when she was silent, he knew she'd be there without a second thought if he reached out. He'd really never stopped thinking of her as a friend.

Well, that was it. He just had to remember that she wasn't his enemy, and he could go back to the enemies-to-lovers trope. It wasn't really about him and Bis. It was about his characters. They could hate each other all they liked. It didn't even need to be any good. Schuyler would help whip it into shape. All he needed was to put words on the page and give her enough pages that they could make something out of it.

Plucking his phone from the desk, he pulled up her name and pressed the green call button.

"You have an idea yet?" she said by way of hello.

"Kind of," he sighed. "I'm looking to you to polish this turd into a diamond, I hope you know."

"Don't I always?" She cackled, and he huffed unamused. "What's it about?"

"Well, I started with enemies-to-lovers—"

"Good."

"—but then I got distracted, and they started having sex too early."

"Even better."

"No, it's not." Bo groaned and leaned back in his chair. "I already deleted the sex scene."

"You wrote a sex scene and then deleted it? I should drop you right now."

He blew out a breath. "I wrote it then figured I could use it later in the story, so I moved it to a new document to come back to it. It felt wrong having them go through something so intimate at such a volatile time in their relationship."

"Understandable," she said, cursing at someone on her end of the phone before returning to their call. "What're their names?"

"Grace and Ryan," he said, typing absentmindedly while he spoke, tucking the phone between his ear and shoulder. "He's a firefighter, and she's a schoolteacher. I thought that he could come onto campus for the kids' fire safety talk every year, so they know each other, but something happened the first year, and they've been arguing with one another ever since."

"Good setup. Have you thought about their inciting incident yet? What caused the spark?"

"I don't know yet. I figured that would come to me once I write more, get a feel for who these characters are."

Bo glanced at the scene he was writing and realized his characters were back to having sex. If he wasn't careful, his removed scene document would end up longer than his actual story. He highlighted the whole scene to move it over when his eyes caught on a single word—Tabitha. He read through the sentence, and his body stiffened in his chair, letting his phone clatter to the floor. He had just been writing a sex scene. About Tabitha. Not his character. Tabitha. He couldn't even pretend this scene wasn't about her since he'd actually used her name instead of the character's.

"Shit!" he muttered and leaned down to grab his phone from the floor. "Sorry about that, but I gotta go."

"Okay, well... send it to me!"

Bo barely registered Schuyler hanging up, too concerned with his computer screen. He wanted to delete it, to start again from scratch, but he was on deadline and knew Schuyler would kill him if he just tossed out word count like it was nothing. He highlighted it again, with the intention of using cut and paste, but his finger hovered over the backspace key. He slammed his finger down, and the entire scene disappeared. He sighed with relief before the guilt overcame him.

Quickly typing Control + Z to undo the deletion, he moved the scene to his other document before he could think too hard on it again.

***

Bo was nervous about dinner with Tabitha. She could arrive at any moment, since Neil's soccer practice started half an hour ago. He didn't know how long their discussion would last, so he'd asked Glenn to pick up his son and look after him, making sure he ate dinner.

The doorbell rang, and his stomach fluttered. He didn't know what to expect from this discussion, but he knew it needed to happen. There were a few questions hanging between them that needing clearing up.

As the door opened, Tabitha's face swung around to face him. She bit her lip, her brow was drawn, and her arms were crossed over her body so far it looked like she was hugging herself. She was ready to bolt. Or vomit. Honestly, it could have been both.

"Come on in," he said, holding the door further open.

She eyed the door frame, like it would hurt her to pass, but stepped through anyway. When she walked inside, she gave him a wide berth.

"I'm not going to bite," he said.

She chuckled politely, but it sounded nothing like her usual laugh. This was mechanical, robotic. Nothing like the boisterous one she usually had, like she was drunk on life.

"Drink?"

"God, yes."

"Right this way." He led her into the kitchen and poured some wine into two waiting glasses. He offered her one, and she took it happily, drinking half of it in one big gulp. "How was your talk with Neil?"

She took a breath and relaxed before his eyes. "It went well. I don't know what gave him the idea, but he seemed to think I hated him. I could never hate him. Regardless of my feelings for... I mean... There's nothing that could ever make me hate him. It was just a little misunderstanding. Everything's worked out now."

Tabitha shut herself up by taking a drink. She wandered away to the dining room and looked at the pictures hanging on the wall. One was from the day Neil was born. Another from a Christmas party a few years back, Selena and Tabitha pressed cheek-to-cheek. One of the whole gang from their high school graduation—Bo, Glenn, Selena, Tabitha, Phil, and a few others. A couple candid shots. A photo from Neil's school pictures. The final photo was the entire bridal party from his and Selena's wedding day. Tabitha turned away when she got to it, and he saw her photographed expression in a new light. She looked miserable, and he'd never even noticed. He saw this photograph every day of the last 15 years and was always too distracted to see past him and Selena in the center of it.

Tabitha opened the patio door to the deck and walked to the railing overlooking the backyard. A cool breeze came through the door, and the looming sunset cast a warm glow over her.

"I've always loved the moon," she said, looking up before closing her eyes, like she was making a wish on it. "It has its own brand of magic."

All at once, Bo understood his nerves. Like the photo, he'd seen Tabitha every day for years, known her all his life, but had never really noticed her. She looked beautiful standing there, and a warm feeling overcame him.

"Can we talk about what you said last night?"

As the sun dipped beneath the horizon, Tabitha lowered her head and retreated into herself. He hated that he was the cause. Her shield was down only moments ago, but she built it back up instantly.

He joined her at the railing and leaned on it beside her. "Please?"

"What do you want me to say, Bo?" Her voice was timid, withholding, meek.

"I don't know," he sighed, bumping her shoulder with his.

"When did it start?"

She peeked at him from the corner of her eye. "Does it matter?"

He frowned. "I guess not. Why didn't you ever tell me?"

Tabitha blew into her hands and rubbed them together. "I tried. Once. At winter formal." She crossed her arms again and folded herself further inward then tugged on the scooped neck of her sweaterdress, like she was trying to hide behind it. "I wanted to ask you to dance but you were in the middle of telling Glenn how you didn't think of me in that way."

"Why didn't you tell Selena? She would have broken up with me if you had."

Tabitha laughed then, a hearty honest laugh. This one was real. She turned her head, tucking her cheek to her shoulder. "How could I do that to her? Or you? That would have made me a real selfish prick."

She looked up at the moon when a shiver wracked through her. He should lead her inside to the warmth, but she was right. The moon had created this kind of magic where it felt like they could talk about anything. He didn't want to stifle it by bringing the conversation indoors, but he also didn't want her to go on freezing, so he wrapped his arm around her shoulders and tucked her into his side.

"I'm sorry we hurt you."

"You didn't know."

"But we still hurt you, and I'm sorry for that. And if I'm being totally honest, I'm a little grateful you never said anything back then. I wouldn't have Neil if you had." He rubbed her arm absentmindedly and leaned his head on hers. "Though I'm happy you trusted him and I enough to tell us now."

Tabitha sniffled. He wasn't sure what to say now, but before he could say anything else, she turned in his arms.

"Why is that?" she whispered on the wind, another shiver running through her. She caught his gaze and held it. An inner strength was blazing beneath the surface.

"Because I..." Her gaze was too much for him, too intense, and he looked at the rest of her instead, really looked. The one dark freckle on her nose surrounded by lighter ones. The way her top lip pointed into a cupid's bow. The streak of something near her ear. He swiped his thumb across whatever it was. "You have a little... Is that frosting?"

"Oh, Mrs. D was teaching me to make it... at least she was trying to." She gazed at his lips and licked her own. She must have been nervous, though, because she kept rambling. "I couldn't get it right. It kept coming out lumpy, and then one batch exploded everywhere. I thought I got it all off when I changed clothes, but I guess not."

In that moment, Bo realized Glenn was right. Tabitha would make herself miserable trying to keep Selena's bakery afloat. She deserved more than that, more than his broken self, more than playing second fiddle in his heart, more than a life here in Saint Joshua where she'd never be happy, where he could never make her happy. He needed to find the courage and tell her to go home.

"You don't have to worry about the bakery anymore," he said, stepping back, removing his arms but they missed the contact immediately. But he needed physical distance from her to say what he needed to be said.

"Oh?"

"Yeah, it's time to close." He turned away, knowing this would hurt himself but not as much as it would hurt her. If he believed Glenn, it would be kinder in the long run. "Which means, you can go home. No reason for you to stay any longer, right?"

Chapter 11

Tabitha felt Bo's words like a slap across the face. She recoiled and took a step away, turning toward the yard. Despite her telling Neil she wouldn't get her hopes up, she had. They had risen all the way up only for Bo to knock them to back the ground. He didn't want her—he didn't want to be with her, he didn't want her in the bakery, and he didn't want her in Saint Joshua.

"Right, no reason." Tabitha drained her wine glass and left him out on the deck. Her feelings smarted, and she needed space from him that she didn't think she'd get just from going in the house. She had to get out of there. "Looks like we discussed what we needed to say, so I'm heading out," she called out to him as she made her way to the door. She didn't think she could look at him right now without crying.

He shouted something through the house, but she didn't catch it as she shut the door behind her and hastened to her car. On top of getting her hopes up, she was mortified. She was practically begging him to kiss her, and he made it painfully obvious that was the last thing he wanted.

Winding her way through town, she somehow ended up at her parents' house. Before heading inside, she sat in the driveway for a while and leaned her forehead against the steering wheel. Tears pooled in her eyes, but she refused to let them fall. She wasn't going to shed another tear over that man. She needed to be strong and get on with her life. She needed to go home. Bo had said as much.

Tabitha was accosted with the volume of the television when she braved her parents' house. Her dad must have forgotten to put in his hearing aids.

"Tabitha, is that you?" her mother shouted before the television volume was muted. "That's better. Tabby, are you okay? Bo called for you, worried when you didn't let him know you'd made it home safely. Do you want to talk about... anything?"

"Did it not go well?" her dad grumbled to her mom. "That boy is stupider than a pack mule."

Tabitha crossed the foyer and stepped into the living room. Crafts in hand, her mom wore the same expression when she found out Tabitha broke up with Tommy Mercer. But there was no comparison. Tabitha hadn't even liked Tommy.

"I'm okay," she said, reassuring her mother. "I'm going home tomorrow. I've stayed away from work longer than I was expecting, and Bo decided he wanted to close the bakery, so there's no more reason to stay at this point. Right?"

On the one hand, she wanted her parents to tell her there were a million reasons to stay—this was her home, they loved having her, anything at all. She almost wanted them to talk her into staying, to move back, but she needed them to tell her to leave, to get some space. It was needed now more than she'd needed it when she first moved to New York 10 years ago. Her mother's advice was just the thing she'd needed then.

Her mom set her craft on the sofa, stood up, and crossed the room. She grabbed both of Tabitha's cheeks and kissed her forehead. "He's an idiot, and you deserve better."

"You're not getting married again, are you?" her dad teased from his chair. "I'm still paying off the last one, and you know you didn't love any of them boys."

Her father's words made her laugh, so unexpectedly that she honked like a goose in the process. "No, Dad. That's it for me. I'm done."

"Oh, Honey. Don't—"

"Mom." She gave her mom a stern glare, and her mom zipped her lips. "I'm going to bed. I don't want to talk to him, but if Bo calls again—"

"I'll tell him you're safe, and he can stop calling."

"Thanks, Mom."

She kissed her mom's cheek, walked over to kiss her dad on the top of his head, and climbed to her room. Her clothes were left haphazardly around the room from when she changed earlier in the evening, and she decided now was as good of time as any to pack.

When everything she brought down to Georgia with her was back in the suitcase, she picked up a framed photo of her and

Selena. It was taken at one of their many sleepovers, back before Selena and Bo had gotten together. She and Selena were hugging each other, cheeks pressed together. They had just braided each other's hair and had had a dance party, so they were both glistening with sweat. In the background, Bo waved from his bedroom window, a dorky smile on his face, like he'd had when he danced along with them. The thing that captured her attention the most, however, was that she wore the biggest smile she'd ever seen herself wear. She had been so happy then.

And she wondered if she'd ever be that happy again.

***

Tabitha couldn't live with herself if she left for New York without saying goodbye to Neil, so she took a detour on the way to the airport to the school. When he walked into the administration office and saw her, he gave her the biggest smile.

"Hey, Bis, are we playing hooky? I didn't bring my stuff, but I can go grab it from my locker."

"No, we're not." She crossed the small space to him and put

her hands on his shoulders. It always surprised her how much taller he was every time she saw him. He was almost a man now. One day soon, she would look at him and notice her neck was craned all the way back. "I wanted to see you before I went home. I need to get back to work, and your dad seems to have everything on the home front under control again."

The smile slowly drained from his face. "You're leaving? But I thought you and Dad talked last night. I thought you—"

"We did talk, and we decided that the bakery should close. I'm sorry, Little Bit, but we can't keep it open any longer."

"But what about you two? Didn't you tell him that you still love him? Bis, you can't leave."

Tabitha sighed and pulled him into a hug. "You know that I am always here for you. Whenever, okay? You're my guy, and nothing's going to change that, but I have to go home now. Your dad and I, we were never going to work, and that's alright. I've come to terms with it."

"I hate that you live so far away." He pulled back to look at her face. "I'm going to miss you."

"I'm going to miss you, too, Little Bit," she said, straightening his shirt. "We still have our weekly chats, right? And you can always call me anytime in-between. You don't have to wait for them."

Neil nodded and hugged her again. Part of her didn't want to let go, but she knew someone here had to be the adult. It might as well be her.

"Alright, kiddo. Get back to class, and we'll talk soon."

"Bye, Bis." He meandered back into the hallway and disappeared.

Tabitha was in a daze the entire drive to the airport. She completed the trip on autopilot. She didn't really become aware of her surroundings until she reached baggage claim in New York. After collecting her suitcase, she texted her ride she was ready and headed toward passenger pickup. She had asked her friend to pick her up before she'd bought her ticket last night, and now she wished she'd taken a taxi. She wasn't ready to be around people yet and wouldn't be able to fake a good mood.

When she stepped into the cold spring air, she almost immediately saw her ride. She was grateful since she hadn't packed a jacket as it wasn't nearly as chilly in the South. The black SUV pulled up in front of her, and her friend trudged down from the driver's side.

"Oh, no. You're sad. What part of him do I need to cut off?" Schuyler asked pulling her into a quick hug. "A pinky? A leg? His dick?" She wiggled her eyebrows at the ridiculous suggestion. "I don't care if he is my client, I will go biblical on his ass."

That was the thing about Schuyler that Tabitha loved—she knew how to force a laugh. When they met years ago, at a celebration for one of Bo's books becoming a bestseller, they instantly took a liking to one another. When they realized they both lived in New York, they became fast friends. No one could ever replace Selena for her, but Schuyler was a damn good friend in her own right.

Schuyler tossed the suitcase into the trunk and hiked back into the driver's seat. When Tabitha crawled inside, Schuyler handed her an orange and white bag, the sight of which made her extremely happy.

"You brought me cheesecake?"

"You came home awfully sudden. It sounded like you needed it. Plus, I'm not good with emotions. The cheesecake can cheer you up far better than I can."

Schuyler drove like a maniac, zipping back and forth through the lanes like she was playing a video game. "Eat shit and die!" she yelled suddenly at a car who cut her off.

While Schuyler drove and swore at the other drivers, Tabitha ate her dessert in contemplation. "You think he knows we're friends?"

"I don't know why he would unless you told him."

"You haven't mentioned it?"

"No, my clients have no right to my personal life," Schuyler said calmly before flipping the bird to the elderly driver beside us. "I may have met you through him, but you're my friend. He's just my client. There's a difference."

"Awe, shucks." She managed to give her friend a lopsided grin.

The car had barely stopped in front of Tabitha's building when Schuyler threw it in park. "What now?"

"I get my bag from your trunk, climb five flights of stairs, and take a nap."

"You know that's not what I mean." Schuyler gave her a no-nonsense look.

"I'm looking forward to everything getting back to normal." She blew out a breath. "I let myself get caught up down there and hoped for things I knew weren't going to happen. It's time to go back to work and stop thinking about him."

"You need to get laid." Schuyler wiggled her eyebrows, and Tabitha laughed with her. "You know what they say. 'The best way to get over someone is to get under someone else.'"

"If I get to that point, I'll let you know. We can go out together. You can be my wing woman."

"Deal."

Tabitha said her goodbye, grabbed her suitcase, and climbed the stairs to her apartment. Closing the door behind her, she blew out a breath. The place was eerily quiet. Everything was exactly where she'd left it, but it felt different somehow. So still and empty. Her apartment had never felt this lonely before. It almost felt like her apartment knew it was no longer her home.

Chapter 12

That evening, Bo made dinner for Neil, but his son refused to speak, giving him the sullen teenager silent treatment. When he first came home, after his soccer practice, Neil yelled at him, rightly assuming Bo was the reason Tabitha left. He couldn't remember a time when Neil had ever yelled at him or said an unkind word. Neil's ranting had left Bo speechless, but then his son fled to his room. Admittedly, he should have prepared for some hurt and anger. He was feeling the same. And guilt. And shame. He hated what he'd said to Tabitha, so he couldn't find it in himself to excuse himself while being put on the spot like that.

When he called Neil down for dinner, he expected more

yelling, but his son had been eerily silent. He'd said his piece. Bo knew he was still upset and wondered how long he'd have to hold up the conversation by himself.

"You know..." Bo grumbled, pushing his food around with his fork. "She didn't even tell me she was leaving."

He looked up, but Neil kept his eyes on his plate, like he hadn't heard.

"She was never going to stay, Neil. She has a life and a job up in New York. She needed to get back to it."

Bo set his fork down and wiped his mouth with his napkin. He stared at his son waiting for anything, a sign he was listening. When Neil slipped and looked up at him, Bo tried again.

"She was never going to be happy here."

Neil gave him an exasperated roll of the eyes, like only a teenager could do. "Do you know what Bis said just yesterday? She told me she still loves you but that you could never love her like you did mom."

"She's right."

Neil flinched, and Bo felt a pang of guilt.

"But... it's Bis. How can you not love Bis?"

"I never said I didn't, but I can never love her like I love your mom. I just can't. It'll never be the same."

"So, you do love Bis?" Neil's lips pulled into a grin, one that Bo didn't like.

"I never said that either." Bo was getting verbal whiplash from this conversation. "I feel like we're going around in circles."

"I think I got it," Neil announced. "You can't love her like Mom because for some reason that you won't say, and you also won't admit to loving or not loving Bis. Yep, crystal clear. For someone who writes words for a living, you should be better at using them."

"Neil..."

"I'm serious. Why can't you love Bis the way you loved Mom?"

"I just can't. Nobody will ever be your mom."

"Well, duh, everyone's different. You can't love every person the same because nobody is the same. I don't love you the way I love Uncle Glenn, and I don't love Bis the same way I love Amber—Don't ask; I don't want to talk about it—but that doesn't mean I don't love all of you, even if you are being stupid right now. Do you think you can be in love with Bis, like at all, even if it's different than how you were in love with Mom?"

Bo leaned back in his chair. He had missed the moment his son became so wise, though that wasn't a surprise considering where his head had been the past three years. Neil had grown thirty years in the span of one conversation.

And he'd given Bo something to consider seriously.

***

Over the next couple of days, Bo had sat down to write the next piece of his novel only to end up writing what could only be described as erotica. On more than one occasion, he unwittingly changed the name of the characters to those of him and Tabitha. In fact, his removed scene document had grown twice as long as his work-in-process and included only dirty scenes. It was more than a little disconcerting how much his mind wandered while he wrote. He'd only ever written clean, closed-door romances before. He needed to get his head on right because his fans wouldn't be happy if they picked up a book expecting a sweet romance and ended up with smut.

His phone rang beside him, and he realized it must have been later in the day than he thought. It was time for Schuyler's daily check-in.

He knew he could stop them by sending her what he did have, from the original story, not the dirty bits and pieces, but her calling everyday helped him flesh out the story. If only the characters behaved on the page like they discussed over the phone.

"It must be three o'clock," he said into the phone. "Hello, Sky."

"Why haven't you sent me anything? I should at least have the first three chapters by now."

On his computer, he flipped windows to the original story and scrolled down. There were only three chapters, and if he were honest, they weren't very impressive. He desperately didn't want to show them to anybody, but especially not to Schuyler.

"I'm not sure they're ready. Plus, they're probably going to change once I figure out the characters further."

"I think you are chicken shit and need to get over yourself. I'm not expecting The Notebook over here. I need to see that you're writing."

"Oh, I'm writing... just not what you want."

135

"You have no idea what I want," she grumbled, though not for him to hear. "Send me everything, the deleted-scene document, too. You need a fresh pair of eyes, and I need to know you aren't yanking my chain."

"Sky—"

"No. You allowed yourself to fall behind at home. You allowed yourself to fall behind on deadline. You don't get to argue with me on this. Send me the documents right now, or I will fly down to that Podunk town right now. Email them to me, and I'll look them over and see what I can do."

Bo knew when to shut up and listen. He opened a new email, attached the two documents, and winced when he hit the send button.

"Got it. Let me pull it up," she mumbled. "Oh! You're document is so long. This has to be more than three chapters."

"It's not."

"What? But it's... Oh! Oh, my. This is the deleted scenes doc, isn't it? Huh. There's quite a bit of them." Her voice grew increasingly excited.

Bo rubbed his forehead and cringed. "I know."

"But it's not bad."

He sat up. "What?"

"It's quite good," she practically cooed. "It's really good actually. Oh, except for the constant name changes. Did you mean for your characters to have an orgy or were you just distracted?"

Bo fell back into his desk chair. "I know, okay? I was distracted because Tabitha was here, but now she's gone, so I can concentrate again."

"Can you? What have you written since she left?"

Bo slammed his mouth shut. He didn't want to answer because the truth of the matter was that his problem had only gotten worse. She was all he could think about and kept popping up in his story.

It was maddening.

"Nothing but sex, am I right?" Schuyler's voice sounded cocky. "Why don't you integrate some of these? They're really quite good, very well written—Oh! That sounds fun." She giggled, and Bo swore he could hear her blush through the phone.

"They're not really my brand," he said, flipping back to the removed-scene document on the computer and rereading a few of the scenes. From a critical perspective, he hated them. But when he separated himself from the work, he could see what she saw. The writing wasn't half bad.

"We can rebrand you," she said. "Besides, if you're really quitting, it doesn't really matter what your final book is, does it?"

Her words smarted. He'd forgotten he wanted to quit. As much as he was annoyed that he couldn't seem to write within his planned outline, he realized he was having fun when he let his characters do what came naturally to them.

"It doesn't have to be my final book," he said, trying to sound nonchalant. "I mean, if the readers like it of course."

"God, you are obtuse." Schuyler cackled through the phone. "Yes, you can write more. Nobody said you had to stop. Yes, we can rebrand if that's what you want. But I want you to think about something for me."

"What's that?"

"Every book you ever wrote had an inspiration behind it— your love of Selena. I don't need to convince you that your new scenes have inspiration as well, frankly because I'm staring at the name right in this document."

She paused, and he agreed—Tabitha had influenced his writing more than he wanted, but he couldn't fault her for it. That wasn't on her. It was on him.

"When you write these scenes, are your characters falling in love or are they banging one out? If it's erotica, if they're just having sex for the sake of sex, we can rebrand for that. But if it's something else, if it's a steamier romance, it doesn't require a full rebrand. We would just market the book a bit differently, but not much would change. You could go on writing books under a steamy romance subcategory. But you need to decide what you want."

That was the question he needed answered. Not just for his story, but for himself. And Neil. And Tabitha.

"Let me reframe the plot with some of these scenes, and I'll get back to you in a few days."

"I'll give you three before I bug you again," Schuyler said, ending the call.

Releasing a pent-up breath, Bo scrolled to the top of the removed-scene document and started reading. Whenever he moved something to this document, he was too concerned about whether his characters should be getting frisky or how he didn't want Tabitha involved in his writing, not whether any of it was even good writing. As he neared the end of the document, not only did he realize it wasn't half bad, but something much more important.

He had an answer for Schuyler and Neil and, though she hadn't asked him outright, Tabitha.

CHAPTER 13

When Tabitha arrived home after getting off work for the day, she was exhausted, unhappy with her job for the first time since she was an intern. The worst part was she had no control over her own designs. She loved creating things but had no say whether her designs were chosen or even if Antonio made alterations to them. While crumpling into her sofa, she dreamed of the day when she could make those choices for herself.

She used to daydream with Selena when they were in high school. Selena would go to culinary school while Tabitha would study at SCAD just two hours away. Then they'd open up shop next door from one another so they could pop back and forth and never be apart. Selena would sell cupcakes and cinnamon rolls by day and make wedding cakes by night, and she could design everyday pieces to sell in her boutique but make custom pieces in the back, like bridal gowns. Selena would get so excited that they would dominate the wedding season.

Her phone rang inside her purse where she'd left it by the front door, she almost let it go to voicemail, but it was the ringtone Schuyler had set for herself—Baby Got Back by Sir Mix-a-Lot. Schuyler demanded Tabitha know it was her because then Tabitha knew to pick up the first time Schuyler called. If she didn't, Schuyler would keep calling until Tabitha finally answered. Admittedly, it was a smart tactic on Sky's part.

"You've reached the McElmore summer home. Summer home, some are not," she said, chuckling to herself, loving how that was how her parents used to answer their landline when they still had a landline. She answered that way whenever she remembered to use it.

"Are you at your computer?" Schuyler rushed out.

"No, but I can be." Tabitha swooped up her laptop and brought it to her bedroom. She peeled off her sweater, kicked her shoes toward the closet, and jumped onto the bed. "What am I looking at?"

"I'm emailing you something," Schuyler said before cursing to herself.

Tabitha pulled up her email, and just as she did so, a message arrived from her friend. She opened it, but it was empty. "You didn't send anything. It's blank."

"There's an attachment," she said.

After clicking on the attachment, Tabitha grabbed a pillow to lean on. "What is it?"

"You'll see," she said cryptically. "Trust me, it's good."

The document opened up to a story that quickly turned spicy, exactly how she liked the books she read.

"Is this from a client?" she asked, stopping herself despite how good the story was getting. "Is that even ethical?"

"First, I've removed all traces of the author's identifying information, their name, address, et cetera. Second, they've removed these scenes from the book, so they're never going to see the light of day. If I told you who wrote them, or if it was meant to be published, or if you took it to publish for yourself, then yes, this would be very, extremely, absolutely unethical. However, I've taken appropriate steps for the author's anonymity, and I'm the only agent you know, and I won't shop it around as your work, so it's only maybe slightly unethical. Bit of a gray area, really."

Tabitha laughed while getting back into the story. She scrolled on down to the next page. This page didn't match with the last. It looked like it was meant to be a new scene.

"These don't match up."

"I know. It's all deleted content, so there really is no consistent flow."

"Ooh, this one is nice. It gets right into it. 'Ryan held her against the door and kissed her, pushing himself onto her core. She broke away from the kiss and instructed him toward the bedroom. He lay Grace on the bed and kissed down her neck. "I've wanted this for so long," she said. "Me, too, Tabitha." Wait a minute. Wasn't her name..."

"What's that?" Schuyler said, using a faux innocent voice.

"Did her name change? Or is this one of those harem stories? You know those aren't my thing."

"I thought you'd like that. Enjoy yourself, but not too much,"

Schuyler said in a singsong before ending the call.

Scrolling through the document, she realized they were all sex scenes. The characters were named Ryan and Grace, but in some of them, Grace's name slips into Tabitha's name partway through. It didn't make sense. Until it did.

There was only one author who knew her. This very author also happened to know Schuyler. He also knew that Tabitha's middle name was Grace, and he himself happened to share a middle name with a character in these scenes.

Tabitha called Schuyler back immediately.

"Holy shit! Bo wrote these?" she practically yelled into her friend's ear.

"I don't know, Tabitha." Schuyler was using a bored-sounding voice. "I removed the author's identifying information, remember?"

"He wrote sex scenes? About me?" she said more to herself than to the phone. "Why?"

"Have you finished reading them yet?"

"No, I just did a quick scan through them, but haven't read through them all," she said, scrolling to the beginning.

"Honey, I suggest you do. You know I don't like feelings, but you have them, so I'm trying to be respectful of those." Schuyler's voice took on an earnest quality, and Tabitha got nervous. "Read them. I'm not sure what exactly... Ryan shares for y—Grace, but you'll see that she doesn't mean nothing to him."

Tabitha's head was spinning. Why would Bo write these? What inspired them? He'd never given her a glance or sign he thought about her in that way. Sure, there was tension between them, but she thought it was because he knew she had feelings for him. Yes, they'd gotten close to kissing that night in the moonlight, but he changed the subject rather spectacularly. Being near him gave her whiplash.

"Tabby, you there?"

"I'm here."

"You okay?"

"I don't know if I want to read these."

"Then don't."

"But I want to read them."

"Then read them."

"You are no help!"

"Listen, I sent this to you because I thought you deserved to see for yourself that you mean something to someone. What you mean to him, I don't know, but there is something there. If you want to read it, do. If you don't, don't. But it's your decision. I have to go now—one of my authors is having a book signing tonight, and she gets really anxious in crowds—but call me later if you want to talk about it, okay?"

"Okay," she said in a daze. "Bye."

"Enjoy," Sky said before ending the call and leaving Tabitha alone with her thoughts and dirty words from the man of her dreams.

***

Tabitha waffled about reading Bo's words. On the one hand, if he wanted her to read them, he would have sent them to her. On the other, she desperately wanted to know what he thought about her, and if he wouldn't say, this might give her some insight.

In an effort to keep her mind off the document, she went to the kitchen for some dinner. It wasn't long before she was sitting in bed, under her covers, a forgotten sandwich beside her, and halfway through the document.

Seeing all the steamy things he wrote while thinking about her melted her heart. Some were beautifully written love scenes. Some were hardcore verbal porn. But the thing was, in most of stories, Grace's name changed to Tabitha during a pivotal moment. There were only a few where Ryan's name was changed to Bo's. Unfortunately, most of the stories stopped almost immediately after a name change was introduced. She wasn't sure what that meant. Did he mean to do that? Did it scare him? Did he want to reenact these scenes together?

Reaching for her phone to ask him, she remembered she wasn't supposed to have this document in the first place. How was she supposed to find out how he felt about her if she couldn't ask about it? Damnit! Why did Schuyler have to share it? Her friend should have known Tabitha's curiosity would get the better of her.

Realizing she could talk to Schuyler about it, even if she couldn't discuss it with Bo, she picked up her phone but dropped it, startled, when it rang out in her hand.

"Hi, Mom," she said into it.

"Hey, Honey. It's Dad."

"Hi, Dad. Is everything alright?"

"Now everything is fine in the sense that nobody is hurt or in trouble," he said politically. It was the way he spoke when he wanted to tiptoe around the truth without straight up lying. 'Honesty is the best policy,' he used to say before saying something so convoluted that someone couldn't help but be misinformed. "However, there is an issue that we need you to come home again and take care of."

Tabitha sat up. "What kind of issue?"

"Oh, geez. Carol, what kind of issue? I wasn't prepared for follow-up questions," he shouted to her mom, probably in the other room. "This is why I shouldn't be involved in these kinds of things."

"Dad!" she yelled to get his attention.

"Yes, Honey?"

"You're holding the wrong end of the phone again."

"Oh, geez." There was some rustling on his end. "Hang on. Your mom is going to talk to you. Bye, Honey."

"Bye, Da—" she said, but her mom had already taken over.

"Tabitha, dear? Since you are a partial owner of the bakery, you're needed to resolve the—oh, what did Bo call it again—settlement of the assets, or something of the sort. I'm not really sure what it's called, but you're needed back here."

Well, that was perfect. She had a genuine reason to talk to Bo, because she definitely couldn't ask him about the book scenes he cut, but maybe if she asked how his book was coming along, he'd admit what he'd written so far. A plan formed in her mind, including ways to steer the conversation to get the answers she wanted. Now all she needed was to figure out when she could put her plan into motion.

"I'll talk to Antonio tomorrow and let you know how quickly I can get down there again."

CHAPTER 14

Since he figured out the plot after talking to Schuyler, Bo had written furiously until he could finally type the words 'The End,' completing the first draft of his latest novel. It needed editing, of course, but he had a complete story just in time, even if it was just the bare bones and entirely too short. He could add detail and setting later, strengthening the word count, but first he wanted to show his agent the progress he'd made. He uploaded the document to a new message and hit send before dialing her up.

"This is Schuyler."

"I just sent you the first draft, and I do mean first. I kept some of the steamier scenes we discussed, and it's a bit on the shorter side since I wrote the bulk of it in 3 days, but I'll fill in the details in a bit. You'll be happy with how it turned out, I think. I have plans with Neil this weekend, so I'm taking a break from it. Plus, I'd like to get your thoughts before I start editing in case there's something that needs a major rewrite or if you want me to add or delete something."

"Hmmm," Schuyler hummed through the phone. He could hear her clicking her mouse. "I'll get on it this weekend. Are we adjusting your marketing or going for a rebrand?"

"No spoilers, Sky. You'll have to read it yourself." For the first time since she agreed to represent him, he got the last word by hanging up on her.

Leaning back from his computer, he let out a much-needed breath. He'd had a lot of confusing thoughts lately and was happy to tick this one task off the list of things to think about. Now it was time to focus on fixing the rest of his life, starting with some quality time with his son.

"Hey, Neil!" he shouted into the bowels of the house. He knew Neil was home but not where in the house he lurked.

"Yeah, Dad?" His voice was loud enough that it must have

been coming from his room.

"I finished my story," he said, closing the laptop and heading for the hallway. "Are you ready? We have to get going."

Neil stepped into the hallway just as Bo reached it, a shit-eating grin on his face. "I'm ready. Have you talked to Uncle Glenn and Mrs. D?"

"Yep, Mrs. D is already there, and Glenn is meeting us once he's done at work."

Together, Bo and Neil walked through town toward the Moon Pie Bakery. They had spoken about it and agreed closing the store was for the best. Today was the last day it would be open, so they were heading over to say goodbye. That, and eat the rest of the stock Mrs. D didn't sell. Neil was most excited about that part. Bo felt all sorts of emotions but knew it was time for a fresh start, a new beginning. Something different to take over the space.

As they approached the bakery, Neil ran ahead to get a start on the leftovers while Bo waited outside. He soaked in the storefront and the sign hanging above that read Moon Pie Bakery. Starting tomorrow, it would all look different. A construction crew was set to arrive in the morning, and he wanted to make sure he remembered it as it was.

"How are you doing with the closing?" Glenn approached and gazed at the exterior with him. "It's a big change."

Bo nodded. "It's time."

"That's not an answer."

Bo turned to his friend and clapped his shoulder. "You're right, but I'm having a lot of feelings about it, and I don't need you to see me cry. For both our sakes, I'm going to take the evening one minute at a time and focus on the good."

"Crying or not, we can talk about it. You don't need to pretend you're doing alright if you aren't. I have seen you cry before."

"Man," he looked back at the sign. "It's sad, yes, but I've done my mourning. I don't want to live in it forever. Yesterday was for mourning. Today's for celebrating, and tomorrow... well, tomorrow's a new day. I'm not really sure what it's in store for me yet."

He led his best friend into the shop for the last time.

Several teenage girls sat in the booth by the window, laughing and smiling. His son had joined Mrs. D behind the counter. While she staffed the register, he took inventory of the remaining goods. After she completed ringing up a young woman with a small child, she came around the counter to hug Bo.

"I'm proud of you," she said, holding him to her tightly.

"Thanks, Mrs. D." He took a step back and pulled an envelope from his back pocket. "This is for you."

Tentatively, she took it from him and balked when she saw what it was. "Bo... I can't—"

"Don't you dare say you can't accept it," Bo said. He crossed his arms to appear stern. "It took some time to calculate the amount, since I had to go back and figure out when you stopped giving yourself a salary, but you deserve all of it. You worked so hard for so long. You need to get paid for your time."

"It can't possibly be this much!"

"Well..." he wavered, "I did throw a retirement bonus on there."

She threw her arms around him in a sappy mama bear hug.

Glenn came around munching on cookie. "You just giving away money now? Can I get some of that?" He waggled his eyebrows then offered Bo a cookie.

He took a bite. It didn't taste like Selena's used to, but to be honest, that was alright. He had to move on, and the first step was understanding not everything in his future would be like Selena would make or do. Like his son had said, everyone was different, just like his love for each of these people was different. It was time Bo embraced that fact.

"Why don't you go talk to her?" Glenn nudged Neil with his elbow.

"Who?" his son asked nonchalant, stuffing a full cookie into his mouth.

"'Who' he says. That girl over there who's been staring at you since at least I entered and probably since you walked in," Glenn said, gesturing to the booth by the window.

Bo glanced over, and a young brown-haired girl watched Neil, a shy smile on her face. She giggled at something her friend said, but her eyes never left him.

"She very clearly likes you," Bo agreed. "Go talk to her."

"I don't know what to say." Neil ducked his head. "Last time I tried, I couldn't think of something and practically ran away."

"Just go over there and say hello," Mrs. D said. "You youngsters always make everything much more complicated than it needs to be."

Bo laughed. "You know what they say, 'youth is wasted on the young.'"

"Don't stress, Neil," Glenn said. "It's not difficult. She likes you. You like her. Say hi, make her laugh, and if it comes up organically, casually mention spending time together. 'Oh, you like ice skating; I like ice skating. Let's go together.'" He snapped his fingers with a new thought. "Just make sure her best friend doesn't also like you."

"Christ, Glenn! Don't be a di—" After a second of thought, Bo recanted. "You know what, he's right. You don't want to hurt anyone just because you like someone else. Don't let twenty years pass before you find that out."

"How can I tell that?" Neil asked, eyebrows pulled tight in confusion.

"Uh... Glenn?" Bo redirected the question to his best friend. If he had learned one thing recently, it was that he was not the right person to answer that question. He'd gone completely oblivious to Tabitha's feelings for so long and unknowingly hurt her over the years. He resolved to never hurt her feelings again.

Laughing, Glenn clapped Bo on the shoulder. "Let me part

some knowledge on you Gallagher boys. Come close."

Neil and Bo leaned in, like a football team huddling around their quarterback. Glenn was the leader imparting his knowledge.

"You can't." Glenn cackled and left to grab a cupcake. He bit off all the frosting and spoke again with his mouth full. "It's not always obvious. It was with Tabitha, but not to this guy over here. Be friendly but don't lead her on. Just be a good guy."

Bo noticed the table of girls getting ready to leave. "Now's your chance. They're leaving. Go over there and walk right up to Amber—Amber?"

Neil nodded.

"Amber—and say hi. Then wait a moment. Hopefully her friends will take the hint and give you guys some space."

"Yeah, then ask her what she's doing this weekend," Glenn chimed in. "If she says something dorky, don't laugh. I'm serious about that. In high school, I once dated a girl who liked to make her cats have a fashion show."

"Was that Bis? Please say that was Bis. I would love to tease her about that."

"No," Glenn shivered, trying to rid himself of the memory

once more.

Bo laughed. "He's right though. Even if you don't like what she likes, don't laugh at it. That's mean. If it's something you like doing, mention that. If you find some common ground or if you want to try whatever she likes, ask if she'd like to do whatever it is with you."

"But what if—"

"No, 'what if's," Mrs. D cut in. "They've imparted as much wisdom as they have, which admittedly isn't a lot, and you don't have all day. She's almost ready to leave. Now go. Scoot!"

Neil walked nervously across the linoleum floor while Amber put on her jacket. One of her friends noticed Neil approaching and gestured to the other girls to wait outside. Soon it was just Neil and Amber. She glanced over at the register, and her smile slipped.

Bo realized they were all staring and suggested they start boxing up the remaining goodies. Since it was the last day, Mrs. D used up as stock of ingredients as she could, so there were more goodies made than usual and with obscure combinations— like white chocolate cardamom pecan cookies and peach marshmallow cupcakes. He boxed up what was left behind the counter, separating the treats evenly into several boxes. He wanted to make sure everyone got a taste of everything, especially since these were one-of-a-kind flavors. Each of them would bring some treats home, but he also wanted to donate extras to wherever he could. He knew they couldn't eat this many themselves.

The bell above the door chimed, and Neil bounced back to the register.

"She said yes!"

"That's awesome, Buddy!" Glenn said, offering him a high five. "To what exactly?"

"She said she agreed to walk her neighbor's dog this weekend, so I asked if she wanted company, and she said yes."

"Good job." Bo watched his son and smiled. He was tired of being sad and depressed all the time. He wanted to be more like Neil. He wanted to be happy again.

Glenn threw his arm around Neil's shoulders. "Onto step two. You've secured the hangout, and that's great. Now you gotta ask her on a date, but the good news is it's easy from this point, provided the hangout goes well, since you already know she likes you."

Mrs. D exited the kitchen and struck her son on the arm teasingly. "Neil, be careful of the advice you take. My son hasn't had a second date since his divorce. And he wasn't exactly a charmer before he got married."

"Hey, now..." Glenn refuted but didn't have a leg to stand on in an argument and returned to Neil. "We'll discuss this later."

Neil nodded and turned to his father packing up the goodie boxes. He reached for a cookie, but Bo slapped his hand away.

"I'm almost done, and you're going to mess up my count. I've got it all evenly split."

When Bo finished packing away the treats, he stuffed the donations into Mrs. D's car. She knew everyone in town and offered to drop them off at the retirement community and her church and wherever else she thought to bring them. As closing time came and went, the foursome lingered near the exit.

Bo basked in the sight of Selena's bakery one final time.

"You sure you want to do this?" Glenn asked, concern in his voice. "You don't have to have the crew here so soon. You can still reschedule."

"No, no. I'm not rescheduling." Bo shook his head and

tucked his son under his arm. "It's time."

He flipped the lights off and walked out, holding the door for everyone else. Mrs. D locked it behind them and passed him her key.

"Mrs. D, you are officially off duty," he said. "We appreciate your service to the Moon Pie Bakery all these years and wish you a very happy retirement."

"Thank you, sir. It'll be strange, getting to sleep in past 4 a.m. and spending all day with my grandbaby, but especially driving through town seeing something else here."

Bo agreed. It would be strange, but he had a plan. He just hoped it'd all be worth it.

CHAPTER 15

Tabitha planned to talk to Antonio about visiting Georgia again, but the rest of the label was preparing for the Paris Fashion Week in a few days. Interns and assistants ran between designers and seamstresses and storage closets. The fabric warehouse was in a sad state, bolts of fabric lying around haphazardly, stacking up into precarious piles. One good blow, and they'd all topple over.

They had completed the New York, London, and Milan Fashion Weeks and still had the Paris lag left. Since she'd missed out on the Milan trip, it was imperative she kept Antonio happy before asking to go home again.

In between tasks, she spent time sketching ideas. She wanted to show Antonio she was on top of all her work, despite not having gone on the last trip. Her new designs were different than what she'd previously created for the label—they were more suited to her own style than his—but she hoped he'd keep an open mind about them. They were more like what she'd always wanted to design, what she'd like to wear.

When he found his way to her workspace, curiosity leading his way, she showed him her look book. He flipped through them slowly, taking the time to decide whether it was something he wanted the label to produce.

"No... no... yes, but you need to change this neckline here. It's too... flat? One-dimensional? No... no... Show me another mockup of this design but change the cut. Mermaid will be out next season. An A-line would work better here. No... no... and... no."

She cringed. "Yes, Antonio."

Tabitha had worked hard on these designs and loved every single one of them exactly as they were. She didn't want to see them changed but needed to stay on his good side until he agreed she could return home.

"Good eye, sir." She closed her book and set it on her desk.

"Very astute, as always."

Though he was already on his way out the door, he pivoted on his heel, his lips puckering, one eyebrow raised. Assistants had begun collecting outside her office, waiting to discuss something with Antonio.

"Why are you sucking up to me?"

She froze. He was annoyed; it was splashed all over his face. Her request needed to wait until his mood had lightened.

"Out with it. I don't have all day." He snapped his fingers, and the assistants in the hall scurried away like cockroaches after the lights come on, eager to leave the detonation zone.

"I need a favor," Tabitha said, her voice diplomatic.

"And that is?"

"I know I just got back from Georgia, but I need to go home again to close up a legal matter." Tabitha winced as she awaited the yelling. "I'll be back before the flight to Paris."

Antonio stared at her.

One of the assistant designers ran up to him urgently and held up two dresses. "Antonio, I need a deci—"

Antonio held a finger up toward the assistant, never breaking eye contact with Tabitha. "When you told me last minute that you, a top designer with the Antonio Riviera Fashion House, would miss the Milan Fashion Week, what did I do?"

The assistant designer backed away. Smart man.

She wished she could do the same. "You let me go home."

"Now you want to leave again, missing the final days of preparation leading up to the Paris Fashion Week?"

"That's what I'm asking for, yes. I understand—"

"Tabby Cat, you have two options here," he said, staring down his nose, arms crossing loosely over his chest. "You can either complete every aspect of your job leading up to Paris, go to Paris, then complete every aspect of your job while in Paris... That's option one."

Tabitha swallowed hard. "And option two?"

"You can find another label." Antonio leaned in close. "I need your answer by the end of the day."

Tabitha gave his demand some thought but ultimately knew the right answer for her. She wanted to create her own designs and have her word be the final say. She didn't want to cower to bosses like Antonio for the rest of her life. Though it had been a far-off dream, she decided she didn't want to wait anymore. She wanted to start her own company.

"I quit," she said, and a smile overtook her face. The words felt so right, everything clicking into place. "Yes, I quit."

Antonio's confidant expression fell into one of surprise. His mouth worked like a fish before he could figure out something to say. "You're one of our top designers. I don't think you've thought this all the way through."

"No, Antonio. I don't think you thought about that before forcing me to make this decision." She collected the few personal belongings she was allowed to keep in the office and walked out, leaving a gobsmacked Antonio behind.

***

Her apartment mocked her. It was all empty and silent and openly judging her. When she arrived home in the middle of the day, it must have known. She rarely arrived home while it was still daylight, and the apartment must have known she was jobless.

She couldn't afford it now. New York prices were absurd. After working for Antonio, she wanted to design her own line, but she didn't have any plans drawn up or seed money to get started. She'd have to move outside the city unless she wanted to drain her savings.

Or...

A thought niggled at the corners of her brain. Tabitha remembered the night she and Selena shared their dreams. She had wanted to own a boutique in town, a place where she could make her own designs, where she could sell one-of-a-kind pieces and specialty items. They spent all night imagining the perfect spots around town for neighboring businesses, and Selena was lucky enough to snag one of their top choices when she opened up shop. It was right smack dab in the center of town, close to everything with amazing foot traffic.

While she was alive, her best friend was pretty fortunate. Selena had gotten the guy. She had gotten the family. She'd gotten her dream store in her dream location.

Tabitha had none of those things, but the thought gnawed at her mind, causing an unbearable optimism.

Hope.

It really was a dreadful emotion.

Tabitha glanced at her phone. It was only 1 o'clock, and she had nowhere to be. Since she quit after requesting time off work, she figured she might as well go through with the reason why and pulled out her computer to search for flights. She found one scheduled for the morning and booked it on a credit card, now that she was jobless and needed to make her savings last.

While packing, Tabitha took extra care to pick out her outfits this time. She would see Bo, and she wanted to know—No, she needed to know what his story meant. If it meant he had feelings for her, too, then she wanted to look her absolute best for that moment.

But then doubt crept in. Hope be damned.

She'd been hopeful about Bo in the past, and it never worked in her favor. It always left her heartbroken.

She stared at the inside of her suitcase, wondering if she should remove the nice clothes and pack some comfort pieces, like the baggy sweatshirt from high school that has the rip in the left sleeve that fits her thumb perfectly or the worn pajama pants covered in constellations Selena bought them both for her birthday one year. In a moment of compromise, she packed both, likely nearing the luggage weight capacity.

The next morning, she took the subway to the airport, not wanting to explain this new trip and lack of job to Schuyler yet. Besides, Schuyler might already know what Bo's book meant, and Tabitha wanted to hear it from him, especially if she had to already see him. She couldn't imagine hearing from Schuyler that Bo wasn't interested and still had to see him afterward. That would be a fresh kind of torture.

The entire flight, Tabitha's optimism warred with her cynicism. She didn't think she'd ever been more hopeful or doubtful in her life.

By the time she parked in her parents' driveway, she lathered herself into near panic attack levels of anxiety. She needed advice from her mom or, at the very least, a hug. Braving the world, she climbed out of the rental and tugged her luggage from the trunk, pulling it up the front path.

"Mom?" she yelled, opening the door to be met with deafening silence. "Dad? Anybody here?"

Though both cars were in the driveway, it was perfectly reasonable they walked somewhere. Saint Joshua wasn't so big that a car was always necessary. That was another benefit of smalltown living, not having to take two trains and a bus to get where you wanted to go.

She pulled out her cell and called her mom.

"Tabitha, dear," her mom said, out of breath. Some commotion happened in the background. "How are you, Sweetheart?"

"I'm fine." Tabitha heaved her suitcase up the stairs to her bedroom while she spoke. It tumbled into her childhood room, and she let it lie where it fell and flopped onto the bed. The stars dotting the ceiling made her think of Selena. She shot up to sit against the headboard to lessen the onslaught of guilt she was suddenly feeling. "Where are you?"

"Oh, I'm around."

Her mom shushed on the other end, but Tabitha knew it was not meant for her. The commotion had flared up through the phone, and she tried listening intently, but she couldn't pick out a voice through the din.

"Why are you calling me during work, Dear?"

"Mom, I'm at your house," Tabitha said.

Someone spoke up behind her mother's voice, and she swore it was Bo in the background. "Is someone there? That wasn't Dad... Is that Bo?"

"No, no, it's just me and your father. Shouldn't you be getting back to work?"

"Can't, I don't have a job."

"That's nice, Sweetheart."

Tabitha sat forward. "What? Mom, are you even listening to me?"

"Listen, Honey. I have to go. Love you. Bye."

The line went dead, and she stared at her phone. Of all the times her mom wanted to talk, she didn't have the time now to stop Tabitha from spiraling. She hopped on a plane without a plan, nobody was at the house when she arrived, and now thoughts of Selena were giving her second thoughts on confronting Bo.

What if all he wanted was her signature? What if she came down for nothing? The papers could have been sent to her, after all. What if..

Tabitha took a deep breath. She was getting ahead of herself.

From what she read of Bo's work, he didn't think of her platonically anymore. What those new feelings were, exactly, she didn't know. But they were there. That much she knew, and she had to bank on that if didn't want to fall down a doom spiral.

Besides, added stress would likely give her an ulcer. And she didn't need that on top of a potentially broken heart.

Chapter 16

Bo worried he wouldn't have enough time to finish the remodel. He, along with Neil, Glenn, Mrs. D, Bethany, and Tabitha's parents, were painting the interior walls of the old bakery. It should have a neutral color, but he was leaving all other creative decisions for the new tenant. If it would have a new tenant.

They had done most of the work already. The construction crew had removed the kitchen, leaving a simple room with bare walls. They had also removed the tables, booths, and the bakery display case. Once the walls were painted, the shop would be a clean slate. A blank canvas. A new opportunity.

He hoped it would work.

It was supposed to be symbolic, but what if he was just overthinking it? Would it come across as he meant it, or would she find it creepy? He hadn't considered that before. What if he messed everything right up? Now that he knew what he wanted, he wasn't sure he could go about getting it.

"Tabitha's here already!" Mrs. McElmore tucked her phone back in her pocket.

Tabitha was in town already? He wasn't expecting her so soon but was glad she wasn't avoiding him. That was a good sign, right?

"Well, damn," Mr. McElmore said, looking up the wall he was painting that had a completely different top half than the bottom. "It's not ready."

They needed to finish before she found her way here. They needed to distract her.

"Go on along, son." Mr. McElmore clapped him on the shoulder and gave it a squeeze. "We'll finish up in here. Just take the long way coming back."

Bo glanced around the shop. Glenn and Mrs. D were painting the kitchen, while McElmores painted the main shop area with Neil and Bethany. The walls were almost fully covered.

They could take it from here.

He set his brush on the paint tray and walked over to Neil. "Are you sure you're okay with this? You can tell me if you're not."

"I'm fine. Really." Neil pushed him away, a shit-eating grin across his face. "Now go!"

Bo really underestimated his son sometimes. For being so worried that the bakery might close that he called Tabitha back, he was surprisingly alright with the new direction of the shop. He was downright enthusiastic about it, though Bo suspected he'd miss all the free after-school treats the bakery provided.

"As long as you're sure...?" Bo let the sentiment hang for a moment. "We don't have to do this now."

Neil shook his head, the smile falling away into something more earnest. "No, we've said our goodbyes. It's time for what's next."

Bo grabbed Neil and pulled him into a bear hug. His son only hesitated for a second before returning it, an extra squeeze before letting go.

How did his son get so smart? It sure as hell wasn't from him.

***

While he walked to the McElmore house, Bo hyped himself up, not that he needed much hyping. His heart was beating quickly, sending the blood through his veins in overdrive. He wanted to talk to her, see her really, especially after the way they left things. He hadn't wanted her to leave, but Glenn's warning repeated in his mind that he couldn't hold her back. And since he hadn't known how or what to ask for, he'd pushed her away.

But he did now.

He knew what he wanted, he knew how to ask for it, and he knew he'd do whatever she wanted if it meant she would stay, to give them a chance, to give him a chance. He couldn't pinpoint when his feelings for her had changed, or even if they had changed at all. Not that he didn't love Selena fully, he did, but Tabitha had been a fixture in his life for so long that he realized he probably had taken her for granted in the past and not seen what was right in front of him. Seeing her again had reminded him how much he enjoyed her company. How much she meant to him. How her absence had also affected him.

He had missed her. Deeply.

The sun ducked behind a cloud. He hoped the darkening

sky didn't mean rain was imminent. The others needed time, and he had things to say before they arrived, so he wanted them to walk to the old bakery. Driving would get them there much too quickly. And as far as she knew, they were only going to be there long enough to sign some paperwork. She probably wouldn't try to push conversation, especially how he had left things.

No, they had to walk.

He stopped for a moment in front of the house his parents used to own and thought about growing up there. They sold it years ago when they retired to Florida, but he would always think of it as their place. He couldn't count how many times he caught Tabitha dancing to the beat of her own drum or playing charades through their bedroom windows or playing house together in his backyard treehouse or as she pointed out all the constellations she knew and told him the correlating stories from Greek myths.

God, that girl was something.

Unable to wait any longer to see her, lest the heavens were to open up and downpour on them, Bo rushed to the McElmore house and knocked. The door opened, and then she was there. Right there in front of him. Just an arm's length away, and some hole in his heart closed up. The realization that she'd always made him feel like he was home, wherever they happened to be.

She made a squeak of surprise, noticing he stood on her porch. It was a delightful noise that made him smile.

"Hey, Bis," he said when she hadn't spoken. "Welcome home."

Nerves coiled in his chest. What if she wasn't happy to see him? What if she told him off? Or worse, told him to leave? He'd deserve it. That was what he'd done to her. He'd made her feel like he didn't want her around him at all, and that was far from the truth.

"What're you doing here?" Her eyes glanced across the front lawn, looking for what, he didn't know.

"Your mom said you were here. Want to settle the legal stuff now so you can enjoy the rest of your time?" Though everything was going as planned, a ball of anxiety had taken root in his stomach. Could see right through him? Did she know what he had planned? "Can I walk you over?"

Tabitha nodded nervously and snagged a jacket from a hook just inside the door. Locking it behind her, she faced him, hardly able to look him in the eye.

"How's work?" he asked, hoping he hadn't come up with a plan for nothing.

She took a steadying breath and looked up at him. Her stare was resolute, assured, dignified. "I quit."

Internally, he was screaming in delight, but he tamped that down. It wouldn't do to get off track. He had a speech prepared. "That's a big step."

"Yes. Yes, it is." She bit her lip, nervousness breaking through, and her gaze fluttered away from him.

"What are you planning to do now?"

"Well... I want to go into business for myself," she said, the nerves leaving her. "I'm tired of others determining the future of my designs. I want to make a name for myself."

They walked in silence for a moment while Bo contemplated what that meant. Did she plan to do that in New York? Or was she looking to make her childhood dream come true and make a name for herself in town? Was it possible to make a name for herself in big fashion right here from Saint Joshua? Was that something she'd be open to trying?

Bo shook his head, remembering he had a speech he need

to get out. With his luck, they would arrive, and he'd have said none of it. "I think that's great. I mean it. That's wonderful."

Her lip broke free from her teeth as a cautious smile, and he couldn't wait any longer.

"Can I tell you about my latest book?" He quirked an eyebrow. "I finally finished the first draft, and I think it's my best one in a while."

Tabitha nodded.

"It starts with a woman, a schoolteacher actually, named Grace."

Tabitha perked at the name. He didn't realize when he'd chosen it that it was her middle name. It took him until he was mostly finished before it occurred to him, and by then, he was completely gone.

"She's living her life doing exactly what she wanted to do, except for one day a year. This one day, which happens to be fire safety day at school, she has to put up with this guy, a firefighter, who comes to campus to deliver the safety talk to the students every single year." He faced her. "Can you imagine that? Having to put up with someone who drives you crazy? Absolute bonkers?"

"Yes," she said, a twinkle in her eye, "I can."

"Me too." He smiled at her, and she bit her lip again, fighting her own smile from breaking through.

"Right, so these two have been feuding ever since he started as the school's fire department liaison. But this year, something's different." Bo urged Tabitha toward the park instead of taking the sidewalk toward the shop. He needed more time, and at the rate they were walking, he wouldn't get out anything he'd planned to say. "Then one year while fighting, they end up making out. Neither could explain it, but whenever they saw each other after that, they are unable to keep their hands off one another. They can't control themselves or keep their clothing on."

She tripped on her shoe, and he shot his hand out to steady her. His fingers buzzed with electricity from where they touched.

"So... you wrote an erotica?" she asked, a playful knowing gleam sparkling in her gaze.

"You know, I just learned the difference between an erotica and a spicy romance. I had no idea that they weren't the same thing." He laughed. "But no spoilers."

Tabitha leaned into him and laughed. He wondered how

he waited so long to really see her, because her smile was beautiful, but that laugh could brighten the sky and force away these thunderclouds.

"The firefighter, Ryan, comes to find out the feud began because they had been childhood friends, but when it came to their reunion, he hadn't recognized her, which hurt Grace. She didn't like not being noticed, not being remembered, not being seen. Even though it wasn't intentional, he had hurt her, and he was terribly sorry about that."

Bo turned to Tabitha and made sure she was following. He wanted her to know that he, like his character, was so very sorry for hurting her over the years.

She nodded, and he took that as a good sign.

"Well, during all of this—the arguing, the fighting... the fucking—the firefighter realized something about himself. He was a miserable bastard, all the time, with everyone, except when he was with Grace. It didn't matter what they were doing, if they were doing it together, he was happy. And he so desperately missed being happy."

As they neared the end of the loop around the park, Bo stopped them before they got too close and kept her from seeing the shop. He had put so much thought and planning into this moment, and he wanted it to be perfect.

"He didn't know when, but somehow Ryan had fallen in love and decided he would do anything in the world to make Grace happy."

He took a breath and reached out for her arm, squeezing it comfortingly.

"What I'm trying to say, in my own weird way, is that I will forever regret not knowing how much I hurt you. Though it was unintentional, you still experienced all that pain, and I am very, truly sorry."

Tabitha's eyes sparkled with unshed tears.

His hand slid down her arm to intertwine with her fingers. "And I hope you'll give me—us—a chance because... I... well, I like you, Tabitha Grace McElmore."

CHAPTER 17

Tabitha stared at Bo, her brain failing to process what he'd said. She knew all the words individually, but as a whole, they wouldn't compute. It was what she wanted to hear, what she'd always hoped he would say, but they didn't make a lick of sense.

He liked her? He liked her? He liked her?

No matter how emphasized the words in her mind, her synapses were misfiring from information overload.

A worried expression crossed his face. "Tabitha? Bis? Did you hear me?"

"I'm sorry. Could you repeat that? I think I just hallucinated."

Bo chuckled, and her brain misfired again at the sound. It

was a sound created with a particular coding, one with direct access to short-circuit her higher brain function. She could get high on his laugh.

"I said..." He tugged on their entangled hands, and she stumbled forward. His arm caught her when she lost her footing. "I like you. You mean a lot to me, and I would do anything to make you happy."

The warmth being in his arms gave her was intoxicating and caused gooseflesh to prickle up and down her arms and electricity to run down her spine. He was saying all the right things, so she didn't even need to confront him, to ask about his book, to seek out answers. After the pain of the last twenty years, it all felt like it was too easy. She braced herself for the other shoe to drop.

I like you, but I only have three months to live. I like you, but...

"Come," he said, tugging her toward the bakery. "I have a surprise for you."

The sign had been removed from above the door, and something was hung up inside to cover the windows. It really was done and gone. Selena's bakery, her dream, was over. A pang of hurt struck her, but eased when Bo squeezed her hand. Choosing to believe Bo didn't have a but, she followed him through the door.

Seeing the empty space, the soft white walls, her stomach dropped. It was all gone. The tables. The booths. The pastry display. It was unrecognizable from the bakery she knew and loved.

"What happened?" She glanced around the room with a tightness in her chest before focusing back on him. "How is it all just gone... already?"

His gaze watched her patiently. There was a resolution there, something firm and unwavering. "We tore it down."

"We?"

"Me, Neil, Glenn, Mrs. D, your parents. Bethany even helped a bit." Bo was leaning forward, anxiety laced through his entire body.

The realization struck her like a lightning bolt. He was nervous. But that didn't seem right to her.

"So that was you I could hear when I was talking to my mom?"

He let out a nervous huff and rubbed the back of his neck. "Yeah, she was here."

"So what they said, about the settlement of the assets, that was...?"

"Technically..." he said with a cheeky grin, "a lie."

She rolled her eyes but squeezed his hand, because she could squeeze his hand now. That was a thing she was allowed to do, and by the smile it put on Bo's face, it was also encouraged.

"Is that even a thing, then, the settlement of the assets?"

"Not sure. It could be," he said, leading her around the room. "They said that to get you back here so I could show you this. Since we sold off the kitchen equipment, there's some money that you, as an investor, are owed. But since the bakery didn't own the shop, only rented, I caught up on the rent and prepaid the next three months."

She walked further into the empty space, their connected fingers hanging in the space between them, and imagined all the things the shop could be. "What are you planning on doing with it?"

"It's yours."

Tabitha's gaze snapped to his. His expression was veiled, and she didn't like that. She liked how he had open and smiling earlier. It made her insides feel gooey when he smiled at her. She could get used to that feeling.

"Mine?"

He rubbed the back of his neck again and shrugged. "I know you wanted to open your own boutique in town. I get that you have a life in New York, and I would never dream of asking you to leave it, but I needed a grand gesture. We tore it down to the studs, and now it's ready for you, if you decide you want it. I have a few suggestions," he led her further into the space, gesturing toward what used to be the kitchen, "like turning the kitchen into a sewing station or office or both and having some changing rooms in this corner over here—but you can do whatever you want with it. It's yours."

His nervousness fell away, and in its place, excitement remained. He had thoughts and plans and hopes.

Hope.

Maybe she could let herself hope a little, too. That he really wanted this, them, her. That this could happen. That she could have everything she'd ever wanted.

"You're giving me a boutique?"

"I'm giving you the opportunity."

"And why's that?"

He tugged her close and tucked a flyaway hair behind her

ear, letting his thumb brush against that sensitive spot on her jaw. "Because I have feelings for you and want to explore those feelings with you, but I don't want to hold you back or make you give anything up. However, I don't want you to think that you need to be with me to get the boutique. You don't! Not at all. I just wanted to give you a choice. You know, maybe you could be happy here. Not that I think you're unhappy in New York or that I'm what could make you happy. I mean, I could probably be happy in New York, which is basically the Mecca of literature, but I couldn't move until Neil is out of school and that's another, what, four years, but really, what is four years in the grand scheme of things? We could do long distance if that's what you want, if I'm what you want. I know you said you used to have feelings for me, and I don't want to be presump—"

Tabitha had decided she'd had enough. She tugged him forward with one hand and used the other to guide his lips to her own. There was a breath of hesitation to give him the time to pull away, and when he didn't, she allowed herself to do something she'd waited her whole life to do.

She kissed the boy next door. The man of her dreams. The

author of some of her favorite new smutty fantasies, and she would have fun reenacting his deleted scenes with him. He wrote with passion. He loved with passion. He fought with passion. She wanted to experience all of that with him.

But nothing could have prepared her for the moment his lips touched hers.

Kissing Bo breathed life into her lungs, sending shockwaves through her entire body. Simultaneously, she had the overwhelming feeling of coming home and the excitement of losing herself. She let her lips say everything she'd wanted to tell him all her life, and his lips answered. As her heart mended itself, the life-changing, soul-wrenching, body-scorching kiss came to its conclusion. She basked in the moment, that perfect moment after a first kiss when the possibilities are endless.

"I hope you don't mind, but I needed you to shut up. For someone so good with words, you also kind of suck at them."

His forehead rested against hers, and a smile tugged at her lips. She opened her eyes slowly to find him staring back at her.

"I'm pretty much only good at words when I can write them down. They're much easier when I can change them when I use the wrong one."

"I bet."

"I give you blanket permission anytime you want to shut me up." His eyes twinkled with mischief.

"Good to know." She bit her lip and glanced at his lower lip, wanting to lean forward and take it between her teeth for a re-peat performance.

"So... what are you thinking?" He straightened to his full height, but his arms stayed right where they were around her waist.

When had they moved there?

"I'd give it a 9, but the Russian judge is only going with a 6.5," she said, feeling cheeky.

"The... what? What are you talking about?"

"Your kissing skills. They're top-notch, not gonna lie, but everyone could use some improvement." She quirked her lip so he knew not to take her seriously.

He huffed a laugh and squeezed her hips. "You irritating woman."

"I hope you know I'm not going to get any less irritating."

"I wouldn't dream of it." He pulled her close, tucking her head beneath his chin. "What do you think about everything?"

"I think..." She snuggled into him. "I like holding your hand, almost as much as I like kissing you, which makes me think I'm going to love—"

"Hey, now." He pinched her side.

She leaned back so she could make eye contact, letting him see the weight of her words. "On a serious note, I think this is the sweetest thing anyone has ever done for me. I think that since I quit my job—"

"You quit your job? When? Why? What happened?"

She slid her hand up his chest and settled it over his heart. "It wasn't what I wanted anymore. I want to start my own line, so this is a wonderful opportunity." She mirrored his words when he gifted her the shop, but nerves were building back up inside her. "And..."

"And?"

"I think that, if you're serious about wanting to explore your feelings for me, I'd really like to take part in that, too."

"So you really do like the shop?" His expression was earnest, which cut her off guard.

"Is that all you heard?"

"No, but it's easier to focus on smaller pieces first and then the bigger picture." He smiled at her cheekily. "In fact, my brain had just begun to process the fact you like holding my hand when you said you wanted to explore feelings together. I was playing catch-up, but now that I have, I'd like to say that it seems we're on the same page."

She glanced around the shop, starting to imagine how she would set it up. She could see it all, where all her designs would fill the space, the man standing beside her, creating a new unit with Neil, not taking Selena's place, but something just the three of them. Finally, it was all there in reach for the taking.

"I agree."

"Good. Can we kiss again, because I'd really like to show that Russian judge what for?"

An uncontrollable laugh slipped out. "Please do."

"Ugh, please don't," someone shouted, startling her.

She'd thought they were alone. "Neil?"

"We've been hiding back here forever. Can we come out now?"

Bo leaned his forehead against hers and groaned. He grazed his lips over hers quickly before responding. "Why are you hiding?"

Neil sauntered out of what used to be the kitchen with the largest grin Tabitha had ever seen. He hurried over, pulling her from Bo's grasp, and threw his arms around her, squeezing with all his might. "We barely finished painting by the time you arrived."

"We wanted to give you both some privacy," Mrs. D said, following the young man from the back room.

Like a clown car, every time she thought it was over, another person left the kitchen.

"Yeah, that was awkward." Glenn popped out and gave Tabitha a bear hug before turning to his best friend. "I'm proud of you."

"Thanks," Bo answered with a sheepish grin sent in Tabitha's direction, and she responded with wink.

Finally, her parents made their way out.

"Well, now that you two have made out—I mean—made up, your mother and I should be hitting the road," her father said jokingly. "If you two go out, be sure to have her home by eleven."

Tabitha rolled her eyes while Bo laughed.

"She's not a kid, Darling," her mom said in her defense. "Stay out as late as you want."

Bo wrapped his arm around her shoulders and tucked her into his side, laughing at her ridiculous parents. "I'll take great care of her, Mr. and Mrs. McElmore. You can trust me."

"Don't play into it," Tabitha teased, nudging him with her elbow. "That just makes it worse."

"Yes, you are going to rue the day you ever fell for me," Bo teased her. "I mean, seriously rue it. It'll just be one long regret after another, all stemming from the fact that you like me."

"But I won't be the only one with regrets."

"Indeed, you won't." he said, leaning down for another kiss.

Over the years, Tabitha had already rued that day many times over, but she was done ruing. She was on to rejoicing in the fact he had fallen for her as well, even if it took him longer to get there. She was choosing to look on the bright side. She was surrounded by people who loved her. She had the opportunity to start her own line of clothes in her very own boutique.

And she was just kissed senseless by the man she loved.

Epilogue

One year later

Bo took Tabitha's hand and led her through the town square, breathing in the crisp, early spring air. He had convinced her to close the shop and take a break with him. If he didn't, he knew she would wear herself out with how much she poured into the boutique.

Moon Pie Designs had taken off, and Tabitha was struggling to keep up with all the orders for debutante gowns she'd been getting. When she opened shop, the entire town rallied behind her, and it quickly grew. Tabitha had hired her mom, but the operation was getting too big for the pair of them to manage alone.

They'd have to hire an additional seamstress to get through all the orders coming their way, but he couldn't rush her. It had to be her decision when that happened.

Chasing Fire, his novel about Ryan and Grace, became a bestseller its first week out the gate. His relationship with Tabitha had breathed new life into him and his work. He was so overrun with ideas that he didn't know which story to write next. He did know, while not all love stories were the same, he was enjoying writing the steamier side of romance.

She squeezed his hand, bringing his attention back to her. "I smell smoke."

"Just thinking."

"Does it hurt?" Her teasing smile tore through him.

Since he gave himself permission to feel again, especially for the woman beside him, he couldn't believe he was lucky enough to find such strong love twice in his lifetime.

Tabitha had moved back in with her parents while she set up the boutique. He hated seeing her leave for the night. When he asked her to move in with them, she'd declined. He didn't want to push her, but he wanted their relationship to move forward.

She understood but didn't want to send Neil the wrong messages. He was at an impressionable age where anything they did could mold him. Still, it killed Bo to say goodnight every night.

He wanted to be with her when they went to bed and her eyes the first thing he saw when he woke up. He wanted to argue over dirty laundry and who forgot to replace the toilet paper roll and whose turn it was to make dinner. He wanted it all.

"I was thinking about buying a new house."

That got Tabitha's attention. "Why? You love that house. Selena loved that house. It's where you made a home, a family."

Bo sighed and turned to face her. "I know, but it feels like it might be time." He tucked an errant strand of hair behind her ear. "It's where Selena and I made a home, and though I'll never forget her or stop loving her, I want to spend the rest of my life with you, if you'll have me. I want to give you the house and the life and the family that you want, no matter where that is."

"Bo..." she sighed and blinked back a tear. "I thought we talked about this. I can't move in with you. What would that say to Neil?"

"That we love each other."

"Do you really think it's smart to throw the three of us in a house together? I mean, we're not even married." Tabitha froze. Her eyes got big, and she looked away. "Not that we have to get married. We don't, really. You've been married. I've been married... a lot, and I don't need to do that again. Really. I'm happy with what we have. Honest. Don't feel like I'm pressuring you or anything. I just think—"

He kissed her to shut her up.

When she melted into the kiss, he pulled away and knelt in front of her, slipping the ring her mom had given him at Christmas from his pocket.

"I shouldn't give this to you then?"

It took Tabitha a moment for the daze of his kiss to disappear and her sensibilities to return. "You don't need to propose, Bo. I love you whether we're married or not."

"I know I don't have to," he said, smiling at the little furrow between her brows. "I want to. I want you—and the whole world—to know how much you mean to me. You're it. I thought I would spend my life with Selena, and I was wrong. But while we're both here, I want to spend as much time loving you as I can.

And I just can't do that when you sleep at your parents' house every night. It's not enough for me. I want more. I want you in the morning when I first wake up. I want you when I go to bed. I want you for every hour in between. I want you." He reached for her hand and held it between them, readying the ring. "Tabitha Grace McElmore, will you marry me?"

A tear slipped down Tabitha's face, but Bo wasn't worried. He knew the expression on her face. It only took him 20-something years to recognize it, but he knew it now. It looked like home.

"Please say yes so I can come out," Neil shouted from behind a tree.

Tabitha's gaze left Bo's for a second, flying toward Neil, before returning. A smile broke out on her face, the smile that had been missing at each of her weddings, the one that conveyed true, ebullient happiness. It told Bo everything he needed to know.

Knowing her answer before she gave it, he slid the ring up her finger, kissed her knuckles, and stood. "I'm going to need a verbal confirmation here, Bis. Are you going to marry me or not?"

"Yes."

The word was broken and barely audible, but the affect it had on Bo's heart was all the same. It splintered in the love he felt for her and broke open all the parts of him that belonged to her. His lungs took a full breath in relief, and a smile overtook his face, one matching her own. His body craved hers, just the need to touch her, so he pulled her in for an embrace that he never wanted to end.

"I love you," he whispered as he peppered her face and neck with kisses.

"I love you, too."

He leaned his forehead against hers, basking in the moment, until he was suddenly ripped from her arms. Neil pulled him away and attacked her.

"I'm so glad you said yes," he said, ecstatic. "That means you're finally moving in."

Bo squeezed his son's shoulder. "Not necessarily, Buddy. We gotta talk about where we're all going to live. It's not a done deal yet."

"Hold on one moment," Tabitha said, refusing to give up her hold on Neil. "I never said I wanted you to move."

"I know, but..." He took her hand and squeezed, "I wasn't sure if asking you to move into our house would be romantic. I thought it might come off like I was disregarding Selena's memory or that I'm trying to replace her or that you might not feel special if you move into her 'space.' I'm trying to find the best route for the three of us to move forward."

Tabitha snapped her mouth closed and swallowed. With one arm still wrapped around Neil's shoulder, she reached her other hand toward him, resting it over his heart. "That is so sweet, but you're an idiot. Neil, don't take after your father."

"Yes, ma'am." He stuck his tongue out at his dad.

"I'm under no delusions that you love Selena. I'm pretty clear on that." She smirked at him, so he knew she wasn't bitter about that fact.

Neil nodded and used his thumb to point in her direction. "Yeah, she had front row seats through it all."

"I loved Selena. That house is where she lived, where her family was made, a family that I love, and where she and I spent so much time together. It would be a shame to lose that connection to her. If you both think you'd be okay with it, I would love nothing more than to spend my life in the place where my best friend spent the life that she had with the people she loved." She leaned forward to kiss Bo chastely. "After the wedding, of course."

If you enjoyed Bo and Bis,
keep the story going with Glenn and Schuyler

Available only from Sapphire Collective Publishing

October 2025

ALSO BY
MAUREEN MARQUETTE

Turn the page for an excerpt from
"DON'T TRUST THE EX IN CABIN 6"

A sweet second-chance, forced-proximity, holiday romance between ex-spouses in a cabin in the woods.

Available only in *Light and Longing* from Kaleidoscope Author Co-Op

Chapter 1

A typical workday for Chloe Danvers looked like a tornado had blown through her office as she ran around like a panicked stockbroker trying to sell, sell, sell. She'd been warned during the interview for her corporate job that it was high-pressure, but she found it only to be that way because of fabricated emergencies and an uneven distribution of responsibility.

As she rose through the ranks, she did what she could to mitigate the stress on the subordinates, but that left too many tasks on her own plate. It was a small wonder she was able to leave the office while it was still light enough to drive the three hours to the small lake lodge where her sister and brother-in-law had planned a getaway for the long Memorial Day weekend.

She hadn't taken time off for herself in years. Since her divorce two years ago, the constant burdens of the job kept her from time spent alone with her thoughts. The 3-hour drive was already more time alone than she liked.

She flipped on her blinker and turned down the winding driveway leading to the lodge. Trees passed by her, masking the route as it curved round and round. On some curves, she caught glimpses of several groups of hikers through the foliage. Rolling into the mostly full parking lot at the main lodge, Chloe's eyes widened. It was bigger than she expected with a large deck built onto the side with restaurant-style seating overlooking the lake. A sign pointed to a road on to the far end of the lot that led around the lake to all the cabins sites. She hoped her cabin had its own parking and she wouldn't have to hike with her luggage to get there.

When she climbed out of the vehicle, the smell surrounded her. The fresh earthy scent of the outdoors rejuvenated her. She was grateful her sister planned the weekend getaway and was looking forward to a relaxing weekend in nature.

Leaving her suitcase in the car, Chloe snagged her handbag and made her way into the lodge. A couple took up the main walkway like they were holding court, so she had to weave around the guests surrounding them. Her foot snagged on the handle of a duffel, and she almost went down, but the bag's owner lent her his arm just in time. Once she was righted, he turned back to watch the couple, and she completed the maze to the counter and smiled at the waiting employee, ignoring the restaurant and activity pamphlets on display beside her.

"Welcome to the Applewood Lodge & Lake," he greeted her, straightening his clothes, despite their lack of dishevelment. "Checking in?"

"I am. It's under Danvers."

"Ah, it's right here. One cabin for 3 nights, with the Price party," he said, eyebrows piqued, awaiting confirmation.

"That's my sister, Kimber."

"Of course." He glanced back at the computer's monitor and furrowed his brow. "May I see your identification and credit card."

Chloe pulled out her wallet and slid the two cards over the countertop.

The innkeeper, whose nametag read Gio, tipped his head

back and forth, as if struggling with a decision. With a determined nod, he slid her cards back to her.

"You're in Cabin 6 in the East Pavilion on the other side of the lake," he said, slipping her key into a paper envelope. "The cabins have their own parking, so feel free to take your vehicle, but you may, of course, choose to leave your vehicle here at the lodge. It will be perfectly safe anywhere on the property, but some guests choose to leave it here for the duration of their stay since we do have security cameras in the lot."

She nodded, grateful she didn't have to lug her bag all the way around the lake.

"The other members of your group are in the other cabins on the East Pavilion, so you'll all be together. We offer activities, such as canoeing, hiking, and bird watching, though access to some of our services and locations will be limited on Sunday for a wedding. You can find a list of available activities for that timeframe in your cabin."

He paused, but Chloe didn't know what to say to fill the silence.

"Right," she said, swinging her purse onto the crook of her elbow.

"If you need anything during your stay, there is always someone manning the front desk. Stop on by or give us a call."

"Thank you," she said, slipping her sunglasses over her eyes and turning to leave. As soon as she stepped outside, away from the throngs of people milling about the lobby, tattooed arms flung around her, pinning her arms to her sides, and her face was shoved into caramel-colored hair. She sighed, exasperated, but returned her sister's hug. "Hello, Kimmy."

Kimber stepped back and smiled at her older sister, her septum piercing glittering in the sun. Though they were raised in the same house, Chloe wondered how they could wind up so different. While Chloe embraced her dark brown hair, Kimber had lightened hers with ombre highlights. Chloe filled her wardrobe with long-lasting, though expensive, garments, while Kimber wore whatever she found at thrift shops. And lastly, Chloe kept her skin fresh and natural, while Kimber was covered in tattoos and body piercings. Though they no longer looked anything alike, they loved and saw each other as often as Chloe's job allowed.

"I'm so glad you're finally here," Kimber squealed. "It's been just us and Trish... and her new girlfriend, Maia. I swear she's been trying to make me jealous since they got here."

Chloe noticed her brother-in-law, Adam, quietly bouncing on his heels behind Kimber.

"Hello, Adam," she said.

They used to be closer since, not only was he married to her baby sister, he was also her ex-husband's best friend—still was, as far as she knew—but their relationship had grown distant since the divorce. She hadn't meant for that to happen, but it was kind of inevitable.

"Hey, Chlo." He smiled warmly.

Memories of the four of them hanging out filled her mind. Back then, she was happy. Though hanging out with Kimber, Adam, and Logan were some of the best times of her life, it wasn't sustainable. The lovely memories turned sour as she remembered how it ended.

Swallowing back the painful thoughts, she turned to her sister. "You invited your ex-girlfriend? Why?"

The concept of staying friends with someone you once had a relationship with was crazy. Sure, Chloe's hooked up a few times here and there, but those were usually over by the morning. As for relationships, she'd only had two serious partners in the past. She hadn't stayed friends with her high school boyfriend, Paul, and she definitely hadn't stayed friends with her ex-husband, Logan.

Kimber flicked her wrist as if Chloe were the crazy one. "I'm happy with Adam. She seemed happy with her girlfriend. I hoped we could both move on and reignite a platonic friendship. I mean, we were friends for years before anything romantic happened. Besides, breakups between queer women aren't like breakups in hetero relationships. I'm friends with most of my female exes. It's the guys who don't want to keep in touch after it ends."

"And you're okay with her hanging out with an ex?" Chloe asked Adam.

"It's none of my business who she's friends with," he said, slipping his hand onto her hip and pulling her into his side. He stared down at her with a loving smile. "Besides, I won."

"That's not nice." Kimber thumped his chest with the back of her hand, but her smile, equal to his in sweetness, belied her anger. "Though it's true. I am a prize."

"Yes, you are." He kissed her so tenderly that Chloe had to

look away.

When they pulled out of it, Kimber grabbed Chloe's hand and led her toward the parking lot. "We're going to finish our walk around the lake—we needed a break from one-on-one time with Trish and Maia. Go to your cabin and unpack, then meet us at the campsite. Hopefully, some of the others will arrive before we make it back."

Adam checked his watch. "Though definitely not Logan. He texted saying he was running late." He looked up to his wife first then over to Chloe when no one spoke. "I'm sure it won't be as awkward as with Kimber and Trish."

"Right," Kimber said. She nodded and gave her sister the biggest smile.

Chloe saw right through it. Kimber knew it would be awkward, which was why she obviously hadn't said he would be joining the festivities. She felt slightly betrayed and like she had been lured there under false pretenses. Chloe loved her sister, but she would have preferred spending time with her without the reminder of her failed relationship smothering her. Getting over him was the hardest thing she'd ever done—nope, second. Leaving when she still loved him was harder.

"Yeah," she said, pasting her own fake smile on her face but glaring daggers at her sister. "What could go wrong?"

Continue the story in

LIGHT AND LONGING

from Kaleidoscope Author Co-Op

Available now